EMILY FEATHER

and the Secret Mirror

HOLLY WEBB

EMILY FEATHER
and the Secret Mirror

SCHOLASTIC

First published in the UK in 2013 by Scholastic Children's Books
An imprint of Scholastic Ltd
Euston House, 24 Eversholt Street
London, NW1 1DB, UK
Registered office: Westfield Road, Southam, Warwickshire, CV47 0RA
SCHOLASTIC and associated logos are trademarks and/
or registered trademarks of Scholastic Inc.

Text copyright © Holly Webb, 2013

The right of Holly Webb to be identified as the author
of this work has been asserted by her.

Cover illustration © Rosie Wheeldon, 2013

ISBN 978 1 407 13093 4

Printed and bound by CPI Group (UK) Ltd, Croydon, CR0 4YY
Papers used by Scholastic Children's Books are made
from wood grown in sustainable forests.

1 3 5 7 9 10 8 6 4 2

www.scholastic.co.uk/zone

For Holly

and Bethan

"Why are you staring at me?" Lory gazed back at Emily over the top of her piece of toast.

"I'm not!" Emily tried to sound convincing, but it was tricky. She had been staring. She hadn't even meant to. She just kept finding herself doing it, to all of her family. Lark and Lory, and Robin, and her mum and dad.

Staring was hardly surprising, though. It was

only a week since they'd told Emily that she was adopted. And not even properly adopted – just found. She was a *foundling*, Emily thought, stirring her cereal, and deciding she didn't feel like eating it. Foundlings were something out of history. That kind of thing wasn't supposed to happen now.

Having your older twin sisters grow wings in front of you probably wasn't supposed to happen either, though. Most people thought fairies didn't exist. Emily had proof – she lived with five of them.

"You're doing it again!" Lory put down the toast and glared. "Is my make-up looking weird or something?"

"No . . . no weirder than usual, anyway." Emily

2

shrugged. Lory liked glittery eyeshadow, but the secondary school had a no make-up policy, so she only got to wear it at the weekends. That meant she spent at least half an hour using every product she could find. Today she had small purple jewels stuck on the ends of her eyelashes.

"Can you actually see?" Emily asked, leaning over the table and peering up under the feathery fan of lashes.

"Of course," Lory said irritably. Her eyelashes fluttered as she scowled, and the purple jewels shook and danced. Emily bit into her upper lip and kept looking as the tiny purple gems grew glittering wings and flew away, humming and buzzing around Lory's hair before they settled on her eyelashes again. Emily wasn't sure if Lory was actually wearing tiny fairy insects as make-up, or if they were jewels, and her sister had just charmed her into seeing them fly.

"Mmmm, she can see perfectly. That's why she fell down the stairs," Lark put in, elbowing her twin slyly, as she slathered marmalade on to another piece of toast. Lark and Lory weren't identical twins, even without Lory's glitter obsession. Lory was blonde and Lark had brownish streaky hair – but even though they were easy to tell apart, there was still something about them that obviously made them sisters. Emily's younger brother, Robin, had the same pointed chin and huge eyes. They belonged together.

The way she didn't look like the rest of her family had been one of the first things that had

4

made Emily wonder why she didn't seem to fit in properly sometimes. She was normal-looking. She had dark, wavy hair that curled on a good day, and always looked like a straggly mess when she got out of bed. Dark eyes that were pretty-ish when she caught herself sideways in a mirror. But she wasn't striking like all the others. Even her dad was beautiful. People were always interviewing him about the books he wrote, and they generally said more about his film-star cheekbones and silver hair than they did about the books he wrote.

Lory looked over at her, smirking. "You stare at me, I'll give you something to watch."

Emily swallowed. "They weren't real, then? Those things?"

Lory rolled her eyes. "I keep forgetting how much you don't know."

"So tell me!" Emily huffed, but Lory and Lark only glanced at each other, and shrugged with an identical twitch of their shoulders. "Ask Mum," Lory said. "Or Dad. Although good luck getting any sense out of him today. I asked him if he wanted breakfast, and he said that was an interesting question, and did I think teeth always had to be attached to something. He's obviously writing another monster."

Emily sighed. "All right. So tell me about the beetle eyelashes. You didn't really just turn those glittery bits into beetles, then?"

"We're not supposed to use fairy stuff here, Ems," Lark explained. She was always more

6

patient than Lory. It was usually Lark who persuaded her twin to let Emily hang around with the pair of them. Now that they were thirteen, they seemed to have got suddenly old, and far too cool for little sisters.

"But Lory made me see them!" Emily protested. "Isn't that using magic?"

"We-elll, yes," Lory admitted. "Only a teensy bit, though. No one's going to complain about that. Mum and Dad wouldn't notice it."

"I don't see why you don't do all your make-up by spells," Emily muttered. "Then you wouldn't always take so long getting ready to go out."

"Because I can't." Lory was obviously about to say something snappish, but Lark nudged her, and she added, quite nicely, "If I did that, it would have to last all day, wouldn't it?"

"Not necessarily," Emily shot back. Lory changed her nail polish four times a day if she felt like it.

"It would be a full glamour spell," Lark explained. "Making you see her as something she actually isn't. And not just you — everyone who saw her. *And* she'd have to keep it going all the time. That's loads of magic."

"Mmmmm." Emily nodded, seeing the difference. "So what would happen if you did that? Something awful?" She frowned, wondering what it would be — the sky falling in, perhaps, or the sudden appearance of a flight of dragons ready to blast her sister to ashes.

8

"Mum would ground me." Lory stuffed the rest of the toast into her mouth and got up, wandering out into the garden.

Emily sighed, vaguely stirring the last of her milk. There was still so much she didn't understand. She was glad that Ash, her dad, had brought her home, all those years ago, after finding her abandoned on the riverbank. Of course she was – she couldn't imagine living anywhere else. But this last week, she couldn't stop wondering about her real parents. Why had they left her wrapped in a blanket by the river? Emily kept picturing the day. Her adopted dad walking along under the willow trees, by the water – he'd told her it was a beautiful afternoon – and then coming across this strange little bundle. Had her real mother been hidden close by all the time, watching to see if someone came across her baby? Had she wanted to leap out and snatch her back?

And what would Emily be like if she had kept her?

"Perhaps your real parents were brilliant cooks," Robin suggested, as he watched Emily picking hot muffins out of the baking tray and blowing on her fingers. Their huge black dog, Gruff, was watching too, edging closer and closer. He was tall enough that his whiskers were already at muffin-level, and they were twitching.

Emily looked up so sharply she forgot what

she was doing, and one of the muffins rolled off the edge of the table.

Robin caught it inhumanly fast, just before it hit the ground, and beamed at her. "It's OK, I'll have that one. Ten-second rule."

Gruff glared up at him. Anything that fell off the table was his. He knew that.

"It didn't even go on the floor!" Emily protested.

"But it was close." Robin smiled at her virtuously. "I really don't mind. You know, someone's got to eat it. Do you think I'm right about your mum and dad?"

"I don't know." Emily turned away to put the baking tray in the sink. "I hadn't thought about it."

"Liar." Robin picked at the wrapper round the muffin. "This smells great," he told her, in between blowing hard at the hot cake. "What's in it? Chocolate and, umm. . ."

"Orange," Emily muttered, sitting down at the table next to him and picking out a muffin for herself. She felt like she deserved one.

"Are you cross with me for asking about your mum and dad?" Robin said, with his mouth full.

"No," Emily sighed. She supposed he must be almost as curious as she was. She looked over at him, suddenly struck by something. "When did you know that I wasn't really your sister?" Robin was two years younger than she was. He had been born after their parents had adopted her, so at some point he must have been told Emily's story.

Robin picked a couple of chunks of chocolate out of his muffin and sucked them, eyeing her thoughtfully. "I suppose I was about five. Maybe six? Old enough to understand that I mustn't tell you. It didn't matter, though. You'd always been there, and you always will be." He shrugged. "I was used to secrets. Mum had a spell on me; she had to. Otherwise I would have told everyone at preschool that I could fly."

Emily nodded, feeling hurt all over again. She understood, but she couldn't help it. It was bad enough that she wasn't born part of her family — or even their people. But they had all known, and hidden it from her. She felt as though they had been talking about her behind her back.

"I knew you were different anyway," Robin

added. "You feel different. Humans do. But I wasn't old enough to understand why, then."

Emily frowned at him. "Why do we?"

Robin shrugged. "You just . . . do." Then he glanced over and caught her lost, disappointed face. "It's hard to explain! All right. All right. . . We're made differently. I mean, we look human now, but you saw how we really look. When we told you the truth."

Emily nodded, remembering. They had shown themselves to her, one after the other. Unfurling wings from their shoulders, spotted and dappled in gorgeous, eye-watering patterns. Their faces had changed, their eyes huger than ever, and glowing with a magical light. Emily had been able to see, even then, when she was completely shocked, that these were their real selves. They had looked *right*.

And so different from her.

"I saw," she agreed huskily.

"Well, we're not made the same way as you – we don't really have blood like humans, for a start."

Emily blinked at him, trying to remember. Had she ever seen Lark or Lory or Robin fall and scrape their knees? Had she ever seen them bleeding? She didn't think so. She had been the clumsy one, who was always tripping over her own feet. . . "No blood at all?" she asked, frowning, staring at his white wrists and trying to see veins through the thin, pale skin.

"Magic." Robin shrugged. "Magic instead.

It's what makes us alive. But it means that we can sense the blood in you, and it feels special. There's a sort of warmth in humans that we don't have."

Emily put out her hand and touched his fingers lightly. They were sticky with chocolate smears, and as warm as they always were.

Robin grinned at her and licked the chocolate off. "I'm not explaining it very well. I feel warm, you know I do. Come on, you'd have noticed if we were all freezing all the time."

"Yee-ees," Emily agreed, considering. She had always loved sitting snuggled up on the sofa with Robin while their dad read picture books or told them his amazing stories. She'd definitely have noticed if her fairy family were cold-skinned.

16

"You have a sort of life in you that makes fairies feel stronger. That's why we've always tried to keep you away from them. They want you." He nibbled the muffin again. "And I guess you've got that even more than most people, because you've lived here, in a house full of fairies. You're sort of human-plus. You've got a little bit of magic in you too; it's just grown into you. And it's stronger since you went through the doors."

Emily nodded slowly. It made sense, sort of. Although it would be nice if she had a little bit of magic that she could actually do something with, instead of it just making her extra-delicious for evil ancient fairies. It was like she was a double chocolate muffin, with extra chocolate chips. And icing.

"So . . . you're made of magic?" she asked slowly, trying to get as much out of Robin as she could while he was feeling chatty.

"Mmm." Robin nodded happily round a huge mouthful of muffin.

"But if you don't have the same insides as humans, how come you can eat human food?" Emily frowned at the muffin, and Robin put his hand over it protectively.

"I still need food! We don't need to eat as often as humans, actually. But I like food." He beamed at her. "Especially chocolate. I think humans stole chocolate from us somehow. They must have done. It's too good."

Emily hardly heard him. She was staring down at her hands, and the faint blue lines of the veins running down them. Ever since she'd found out about the fairies, she kept thinking of other things she wanted to know – and some that she wasn't sure she wanted to know at all. "Are vampires real too?"

Robin snorted. "No. Well. . ."

"They *are*?" Emily gave a little gulp of horror.

"Not the way you think. Not all that stuff with the garlic, and the biting and stupid cloaks. But it's like I said, fairies want to steal humans over to our side, if they can. And the humans, they become sort of drained. Some of the life goes out of them. Especially if they have fairy food. Nothing else ever tastes as good ever again, so people just waste away after that. So you can see where the vampire

19

stories come from." He grinned at her, drawing his lips back. "And most fairies do have really pointy teeth."

Emily nodded, staring at him rather blankly, and Robin sighed. "Don't be all miserable, Ems. I was trying to tell you stuff, that's all. You *wanted* to know."

"I'm not. It's just – it's just all so different. Some of the time it's the same, and then you tell me things like that, and it makes me feel like I never knew any of you. Like I was stupid to even think I was your sister."

Robin looked down at his muffin again, carefully ferreting around for more bits of chocolate. "You *are* my sister."

Emily stared at him. "But I'm not!"

20

He shrugged. "Yes, you are. You've always been here. And you're usually a lot nicer to me than Lark and Lory, even if they do have the same parents as mc." He shoved the rest of the picked-apart muffin into his mouth and looked at Emily hopefully. "Can I have another one?" he asked, spraying crumbs. "Pleathe?"

Emily simply handed it to him. However much Lark and Lory and her mum and dad had tried to explain that they loved her, and they wanted her, and she was special, it had still left her feeling as though she'd been turned inside out and upside down. Robin's calm acceptance of it all – and his greed, which was exactly the same as it had always been – almost helped more.

"Do you think I'll ever know who my real parents are?" she asked him suddenly. Then she took a quick bite of muffin so as not to look too worried about his answer. He'd just proved that he felt like her little brother. She couldn't let him get too big for his boots.

"You could look for them. . ." Robin frowned, his thin, dark-red brows drawing together. "But – do you want to? I mean –" He shrugged. "They did leave you there, Ems. I don't know if . . . well. Maybe you wouldn't like them."

"There must have been a reason," Emily said shakily. Surely there had to have been a good one? Unless they just hadn't wanted her?

A tear fell on to the chocolatey crumbs, and Emily gulped.

22

Robin swallowed a huge bite of his second muffin and eyed her worriedly. "Do you want me to get Mum? She's in her workroom. She said she had an idea for a new design for a scarf. . ." He started to get up, backing away as though he thought the crying might be infectious.

"No," Emily sniffed, shaking her head. "I'm all right. It's just scary – what if I am like my mum and dad, and they didn't care about me at all? I might turn out to be a horrible person too."

Robin wrinkled his nose, thinking. "I suppose so. But you aren't horrible now, are you? Why should you turn into somebody else?"

"Because I feel like somebody else!" Emily cried. "Everything's changed!"

"No, it hasn't!" Robin glared at her. "It's exactly the same, except you know about it. That's all."

Emily stared at him helplessly. *All?* She supposed he was right – but how could he think it was so easy?

Robin chased crumbs round the table with one finger. "You really are a very good cook. And you always knew you didn't get that from Mum or Dad, didn't you?" Their mother's home-made cakes were legendarily awful. All four of the children conspired to hide them at school cake sales, or they had until Emily had just taken over. Their dad didn't cook at all, except for sandwiches made out of toast and anything he could find in the fridge, when he wandered out of his study at three in the morning after wrestling with a difficult chapter.

Emily sighed. What Robin said was true. Then she smiled sweetly at him. "You aren't having another muffin, so don't even try."

Emily made a mug of tea and put one of the chocolate-orange muffins on a plate. Then she headed for her dad's little study, which was cleverly fitted into a cubbyhole under the stairs. Although, thinking about it now, it was an awful lot bigger than it should have been. Emily picked a chocolate chip out of the muffin as she stared at the study door. There must be some sort of spell. The space under the stairs was just a tiny cupboard, really, so how was there room for a desk and a red velvet armchair? Let alone the piles and heaps and wobbling towers of books. Emily shook her head crossly. How had she never noticed these things before? She put out her hand to open the door. Her dad was working, but she reckoned that if she was lucky, with the tea and muffin as bribery, she might be able to get him to stop for a bit and talk to her.

When he and her mum had told her what the family really were last weekend, Emily had been so shocked she'd hardly asked any questions. The news was just too big and strange. After they had told her the truth, Emily had run away from them all, desperate to have some time alone to think. But the house, which was full of doors that led to nowhere, and everywhere, had somehow sensed the eruption of fear and magic from the family argument and shifted. Looking back now, of course, there had been odd hints of something strange about the house long before. Moments when Emily thought she saw something odd in a mirror. The way the clouded, swirly old glass in her bedroom windows seemed to have strange cities floating in it. Her dad's study. She should have known it wasn't just her imagination.

As Emily had raced up the stairs, they had changed into something strange and new. She had thought it was her parents trying to stop her, and kept running, until she burst out through one of the secret magical doors on to a riverbank somewhere elsewhere. The fairy world.

It hadn't taken long for the fairy people to find her. Over the years they had caught glimpses of her through the doors and wondered about this curious human child, almost in their world. Her arrival had been noted at once, and then there had been music, strange sweet singing, and Emily had fallen asleep. She'd woken to find herself in a palace, surrounded by beautiful, terrifying, hungry creatures, the Ladies of the fairy court.

These were the kind of evil ancient fairies who would happily keep human children as pets, as they were so full of energy and life. For fairies, who could live a very long time, the child's youth was a sort of tonic. *Like vitamin tablets*, Emily thought now. The Ladies had tried to feed Emily with the most delicious-looking fruit and berries, but her sisters had rescued her before she had eaten anything.

Emily shivered, thinking about it again. It was like Robin had just explained. She might not have got any older in the fairy country, but she would have been used up. Perhaps she would have just disappeared.

Emily had been making a sort of mental list of the things she wanted to know. She liked chatting to Robin, and Lark and Lory, but her dad was the best at explaining things – it was what he did for a living, after all. She opened the study door cautiously. Her dad could be very bad-tempered when he was working. If he was in the middle of a tricky bit, he was quite likely to yell, or throw a pencil at her. She needed to get in with the tea and the muffin quickly.

Ash wasn't at the computer – he was curled into the battered old armchair in the back corner of the room, scowling down at a notebook. As Emily peered round the door, he scowled at her instead.

"I brought you tea!" She held the mug out enticingly. "And I made muffins!"

"What have you broken?" her dad asked suspiciously. "Please don't tell me it's the TV again."

"I haven't broken anything." Emily put the muffin down on top of his notebook and smiled hopefully. "I just want to talk to you. Ask you things. Please?"

Ash looked at her thoughtfully, and took the tea and the muffin, sliding the notebook on to the floor. "I'd been expecting you to ask before, Ems. I know we owe you an explanation. More of one than you got last week, anyway. I've been waiting for you to be ready."

Emily nodded gratefully, and her dad squashed himself to one side of the armchair, making a gap that she could curl into. She leaned against him, catching the dry, smoky scent that she had always thought was soap, or aftershave. Now she suspected it might just be the smell of him.

"So, are there secret things you can't tell me then?" Emily asked curiously.

"Of course. There always are. Everyone has secrets. But they are things I wouldn't tell Lark, or Lory, or Robin either."

Emily nodded. That was reasonable. Her family's whole life was based on secrets. Some of them would have to be kept.

Her dad took a gulp of tea, sighed happily, and smiled down at her. "And there are some things I just don't know. Mysteries. You're unique, Emily – a human child who has lived with fairies all her life – and who's gone through the doors and come back again. You may have seen things even I don't know about."

Emily leaned back against him, wriggling under his arm so that he had to sip his tea carefully around her. "I don't really understand why you all live here." Emily's fingers dug tight into her dad's sweater, without her really thinking about it. Keeping hold of him. "Why don't you live . . . over there? Why is this house so important?" *And why did you bring me into it. . .* she added silently.

Her dad took a gulp of tea and reached over the arm of the chair to set the mug down. Then he wrapped his arm around her tightly. "It's a gatehouse. Full of doors. To our land, and others."

Emily wriggled round to stare up at him sharply. "Other places as well? What other lands?"

He sighed. "Don't take it as an invitation to go exploring again, Emily. We never meant for you to be able to get through the first time. Most of the doors are closed. Sealed shut. They only open when they must, and even I don't know what's beyond them. But most of the doors are to my own world. This house was built when the town here grew and spread out into the countryside, and the quiet, secret places weren't so quiet any more. It was built to protect the doors. To protect the lands from each other. I guard the house, for the king."

"There's a king?" Emily whispered, her voice suddenly full of excitement. "A fairy king, really? And a queen too?" She imagined a palace, with little towers crowned with flags. Fountains splashing. Games, and dances, and the fairy queen, the most beautiful creature in the world. . .

"No." Her father's voice dropped sadly, and he stroked her hair. "No, our queen died, many years ago."

"Oh. . ."

"Which is why the Ladies are so strong, and so dangerous." Emily's father moved his hand down to cup her face and lifted it up so he could look into her eyes. She shivered, seeing that his own had darkened again, the way they had done when she'd seen his real form.

"They're all fighting for power, you see. There's no queen, and the king might choose to marry again. One of them. Or their daughters, or sisters, or cousins. Everything is about family."

"I suppose so," Emily muttered. Everything always was.

Her father was still staring into her eyes, and even though she tried to look away, she couldn't. "You are part of my family," he told her seriously.

"And I want you safe. Stay away from the doors, Emily." He sighed at her. "I can't believe you've grown so quickly. It seems only yesterday I found you. You must promise me you'll stay away from the doors."

"I promise. . ." Emily blinked thoughtfully. "Are there any others? More doors? Or are these the only ones?"

"There are more. . ." her father admitted. "Not many. And not all of them known. There are secret doors, hidden here and there. The king would have them all sealed if he could, but our world doesn't work well with bars and chains. It needs to breathe, so there are little openings that appear, here and there. The doors in this house are the true gateways, where any visitors can come and go."

"Are there lots of visitors?" Emily asked him, trying to remember people she'd seen in the house, friends of her parents. Had they all been fairies too? Travelling between the worlds?

"Some . . . but not many. Our world doesn't mix well with this one. Our magic is too dangerous. A fairy lost or loose out here is a disaster." He patted her cheek. "And the same for a human child over there, Ems. Only those with permission from the king go through. No one else."

"But if there are secret doors—" Emily began, but her father interrupted, his voice hardening.

"Anyone who uses those doors is a danger, and must be stopped. The worlds don't mix."

"Oh. . ." Emily hesitated. "But, I mean, I used one of the doors, and I wasn't meant to. I didn't have permission from the king."

"And look what happened," her father pointed out gently. "It wasn't your fault but your mother had to go and beg forgiveness from Lady Anstis. Lark and Lory could have been bound over to her as servants for the way they behaved. And who knows what would have happened to you."

"I'm sorry." She hadn't known. She hadn't realized. Which one had been Anstis? Emily wondered. The dark-haired one, she guessed. The one with the beautiful wings like a peacock butterfly, and that perfect crimson silk dress. The one whose nails had lengthened to dark claws when she had come stalking after Emily, as Lark and Lory flew her away back home. "Did Mum have to – have to do anything bad?"

"No." Her father hugged her tightly. "She said it was all very polite. They drank tea, and discussed how difficult it was to bring up children well in this awful place. But we owe her a favour now, Ems, you see."

Emily shuddered, remembering the way Lady Anstis had moved, jerky and strange, as though her legs bent backwards like a goat's. What sort of favour might she want?

"Does that mean I can never go back?" she asked longingly, and her father sighed.

"You want to, don't you?"

"Yes." Emily nodded. "All the time." She glanced up at him warily. "Every time I go past the mirror on the landing, I want to touch it, to see if I can go through. But I don't even see

40

the girl with the greeny-gold hair in it any more. She's gone. Some of the other pictures move, and I still see the doors changing around sometimes. But that mirror's not even misty."

"We changed the guard spells," her father murmured, "when we realized that you could get through the doors. You shouldn't have been able to, but the magic in the house has grown up with you now. The doors know you. And now you've crossed over and come back, the magic is even stronger inside you. Be careful, Emily."

"Careful of what?" Emily frowned up at him, and her father shrugged helplessly.

"Just – be careful." He shook his head at her anxiously, and Emily slipped off the chair, gently kissing the grey wing of hair over his ear.

"I promise I will." It was the second promise Emily had made him, and as she took away his empty plate, she thought to herself that she had no idea how to keep either one.

"Did you understand that homework?" Emily's best friend Rachel asked. "The comprehension? I didn't think some of the questions made sense. It took me ages, and I still don't think I got it right."

Emily stared at her, desperately trying to remember the homework. She hadn't really been paying attention to Rachel chattering as they walked to school. Now that they were in Year Six, she and Rachel walked together, without their parents – except on days when Rachel had been

staying at her dad's flat, which was on the other side of town. Emily loved the chance to gossip about school. The only downside was they had to take Robin with them. But he was running along ahead of them like he usually did, ridiculously fast. *How could I not have noticed how fast he is?* Emily thought suddenly, watching him stop and whirl round, almost in mid-air. *How could I not have seen that he's different?*

On a normal day, Emily and Rachel chatted all the way to school, but Emily realized she'd hardly said anything this morning. She'd been trying to get her head round everything her dad had told her.

The thing was, even though she knew it was dangerous, Emily desperately wanted to go back through the doors. She could still feel the pull of that strange place. Maybe it was enough to have breathed the air? Part of the fairy world was inside her already. She couldn't help wanting to understand it better, that tiny spark of magic inside her.

Mostly, she wanted to see more of the people. Not so much those grand, terrifying Ladies. They had been beautiful – like fairy princesses in books. But now looking back, Emily thought an awful lot of their beauty and charm must be built on spells. Emily was more interested in the others: the tree people who had found her on the riverbank, and the brownie creatures who had worked as servants in the palace. Most of all, Emily wanted to see the girl in the mirror again. She had been the first fairy that Emily had ever seen – apart from the fairies she lived with and didn't know about, anyway. Emily had glimpsed her in the mirror on the landing between Lark's room and Lory's. A pale, curious face, trailing odd greenish, flattish sort of hair. The girl had been looking out at Emily, watching her.

The girl had known who Lark and Lory were, Emily now realized. She'd helped them escape the Ladies' huntsmen, who had been set on them after Emily had decided that she didn't want to be a fairy's pet, that she wasn't eating those strange, oozing berries, and that she was going home with her sisters, thank you very much. The girl had shown them a door back to the house.

A door that appeared somehow in the middle of a river. Emily thought the girl must be some sort of water sprite – she had webbed fingers, as well as that weed-like hair.

"Ems? Homework? You know, that reading comprehension?" Rachel was staring at her.

Emily blinked. Rachel was starting to look annoyed, which wasn't surprising. Even before last weekend's bombshell, Emily hadn't been the best of friends. She'd already worked out that there was something odd going on at home, and she was angry, and teary, and just plain weird – all three taking it in turns.

Secretly crossing her fingers in the folds of her skirt and apologizing to Rachel, she decided the best thing to do was lie. She couldn't remember the homework at all. When she'd got up that morning, school had been the last thing on her mind – again. She'd realized at breakfast that there was homework and she hadn't done it, but Lark had grabbed the sheet of paper and dictated the answers to her in between bites of toast. Then Lory had stared over her shoulder at Emily's homework book and made her change a couple of answers because, as she put it, they were too good to believably be Emily's. The only part of the homework that was actually hers was the spelling, and she could hardly remember the story the questions had been about.

"Mmmm, it was hard, wasn't it. . ." she murmured.

They were just walking in through the school

47

gates when Rachel nudged Emily. "Ugh. Don't look now, but Katie Meadows is giving you the evil eye again."

Back before Emily had learned that there were such things as fairies after all, she and Rachel had decided that Katie Meadows was probably a witch. They couldn't work out how else she managed to get everything her own way all the time, and make everyone else's lives so miserable. She was one of those people who had a talent for spotting weaknesses. Even tiny things, like a bad hair day, or tripping over in PE. She always noticed. And then she found the perfect chance to say something that wasn't just horrible, it was *perfectly* horrible, and it made you feel about a million times worse.

"I think she's got some weird power that means other people feeling awful makes her stronger," Emily said grimly. "She feeds off it. She's like a misery-sucker. Whatever the proper name for one of those is."

Katie was also very clever at spotting the people to pick on. The only good thing about how dazed Emily had been feeling all last week was that she'd been too far away inside her own thoughts to notice the mean things Katie was saying to her. And about her. Katie had several girls who hung around with her, mostly because they wanted to protect themselves, Emily and Rachel thought. If they hadn't been members of her little coven, she would have picked on them mercilessly. Katie had noticed that Emily had

49

something strange going on before anyone else. It was like she had antennae, tuned for it.

"She's got Ellie-Mae and Lara with her, and they're all whispering," Rachel muttered. "We should have gone and found that tree!"

Rachel had read a book about witches that said they could be frightened away with the branches and berries from a rowan tree. It was because there were little stars on the ends of each berry, stars with five points, which were some sort of symbol of protection. Rachel had even looked up trees in the school library and found out what rowans looked like, but then Katie had found another victim, and they'd never bothered to search out a tree. It was probably a good thing, Emily realized. Fairies might not

50

like rowans either. Who knew what might have happened if they'd tried to take rowan branches inside her house? Splatted rowan berries all over their clothes, probably, or worse.

Perhaps Katie really was a witch? Emily shivered. If there were fairies, why not witches too? Perhaps strange creatures were everywhere? She needed to drag Dad away from his book again and force him to make her a list of all the different types of magical creatures. She could ask Lark and Lory and Robin, but she wouldn't put it past them to make stuff up just to see if they could get her to believe it. It would be just like Robin, and Lory was always trying to make out that Emily was her silly little sister. She'd love to convince Emily that there were such things

as ogres, or mermaids, or unicorns. Emily forgot
Katie again for a second, as she hoped to herself
that unicorns were real.

Emily could feel Rachel beside her – they
weren't close enough to be touching, but she
could tell that Rachel was keyed up and waiting,
expecting something horrible to happen. Rachel
minded Katie's bullying much more than Emily
did. Even though Rachel was clever, much
cleverer than Emily, she was useless at thinking
of things to say when people were mean. She
said her mind just didn't work like that. She
thought up the perfect thing to say hours later,
when she'd been worrying over the whole fight
for ages and ages and making herself feel totally
miserable. Emily usually managed to think of

something to say at the time, even if it was only rolling her eyes and telling Katie to shut up.

"You look even more stupid than usual." Katie eyed Emily with her head on one side, like a hungry bird. It was odd, because Katie wasn't the slightest bit bird-like to look at, Emily thought. She had a round, pale face, and her eyes were so dark you couldn't see the pupils. She wasn't pretty, but there was something about her that made you want to look.

"I suppose a whole weekend with your weird family does that." Katie leaned in closer to her, and Emily vaguely noticed that Ellie-Mae and Lara were watching her eagerly, as though they were waiting for something that had been planned.

"You even smell weird!" Katie stepped back, waving a hand in front of her nose as though she'd caught a whiff of something disgusting. "Uugghhh!"

"She does!" Lara chimed in. "Really weird! Like – rotten food."

Typical, Emily thought. Lara was so useless she couldn't even think up a good insult when she'd had time to practise. Emily knew she needed to say something back. Katie wasn't one of those bullies who got bored if people just didn't say anything. She was too good for that. She'd keep going and going until her victim snapped and burst into tears, or tried to run away, or both. The only way to get rid of her was to say something quick and snappy back, and sound as though you couldn't care less.

But today Emily couldn't do it. She had this sudden dreadful feeling that maybe she *did* smell weird. She was weird, after all.

Even your own mother didn't want you, something inside her whispered. *That's what's weird. That's wat they can smell on you.*

Rachel nudged her, expecting her to snarl some insult back at Katie, the way she usually did, but Emily felt as if her voice had disappeared. She had no defences at all. The part of Emily that should have told Katie to go and talk to someone who cared, was curled up in a little ball deep inside her. Without the confidence in her family and her home to armour her, Emily couldn't fight.

"She's crying!" Ellie-Mae squeaked – she sounded excited, shocked, a little frightened. They'd never managed to make Emily Feather cry before.

"Ohhhh, poor little weird smelly Emily," Katie purred, her dark eyes glittering and her fingers clenched into claws. Suddenly she reminded Emily of those fairy Ladies, the way they'd been so eager for their prey.

Emily stumbled as Rachel caught her arm and tried to pull her away. "Come on," Rachel whispered. "Emily, come on." She could hear Katie and Lara and Ellie-Mae crowing with laughter and triumph as Rachel hurried her across the playground.

"What happened to you?" Rachel demanded,

as thankfully the bell went and everyone began to wave goodbye to their parents and stream into the school. She was still holding Emily's arm, and Emily felt as though Rachel might be the only thing holding her up. She didn't say anything, and once they'd got to their classroom Rachel pushed her into a chair and stared at her.

"What is it? What's the matter with you? You've never let her get to you like that before. She's said stuff that was loads worse."

Emily just shrugged helplessly. How could she explain?

"Was it her saying you smelled? Honestly, Emily, that's the kind of thing Robin says to you all the time!"

Emily's eyes filled with tears again, and they began to spill over on to her cheeks. Rachel still thought Robin was her real brother, and it was so hard not to be able to tell her the truth. Emily wanted to, so much. She wanted to talk to someone else. Someone who was *human*.

The way that Rachel was staring at her, the hurt look in her eyes, was even worse than Katie's meanness. Rachel knew that Emily was hiding something from her. Which was awful because Rachel had told Emily everything about what happened with her parents last year when they were splitting up. The arguments. The silences. The way she hid under her bed so they couldn't find her when she knew they wanted to tell her they were getting a divorce. If she could tell Emily things like that, she wanted to know that her best friend could tell her everything in return.

Emily rested her head on her arms and peered up at Rachel sideways. "Sorry. . ." she whispered

3

Emily woke the next morning feeling as though she couldn't actually have been to sleep. Her eyes felt sore and scratchy, and her head ached. She inched herself up in bed, and reached down for the duvet that she'd kicked off during the night. It was another hot day already, but her hands and feet were freezing, and her shoulders were shivery, as though she was coming down with a bug.

Maybe she could stay off school? Emily sighed, imagining staying in bed. There would be toast, and dry cereal, and piles of books. She wouldn't have to creep into school with her shoulders hunched as she waited for Katie and the others to say something.

And she was going to have to talk to Rachel, as well. They'd have to walk to school together again, and the thought of it made Emily feel even more ill. Rachel had been miserable and silent all the way home yesterday. Even Robin, who always walked as far away from the girls as he possibly could while still claiming to be with them, had noticed that something was wrong.

"Did you have a fight?" he whispered to Emily

as they came out of school together in complete silence.

Emily shrugged. "Sort of."

Robin glared at Rachel, but she was staring at her feet as she plodded along a few metres behind them, and didn't even notice.

"It wasn't her fault," Emily added quickly. Robin could be surprisingly protective sometimes, and she didn't trust him not to do something awful to Rachel if he thought she'd started it. He wasn't supposed to use magic, of course, but it wouldn't take much magic to make her tread in something disgusting – quite a lot of people walked their dogs along this road. She gave him a warning look. "Don't. It really was mostly my fault." Then she hurried on, anxious to get this horrible walk done.

Rachel had stopped at their gate, and muttered, "Bye, then," and Emily had sighed and tried to smile. "Bye. See you tomorrow," she added, fiddling with the gate, until Robin lost patience and dragged her into the garden, leaving Rachel to walk round the corner to her mum's flat.

"You'd better make up with her," Robin snapped as they walked up the path. "I'm not putting up with that for the rest of the week. It felt like being wrapped up in a cloud of miserable fog."

Emily had blinked at him in surprise – but then he and the rest of her family did feel things in that sort of way. Now she huddled her duvet round her shoulders, trying to imagine what that would be like. She quite liked the idea. Instead of worrying about *something*, and not being able to work out quite what, you would know exactly what was going on, because there was a sad little cloud of greyness sitting next to you, or wrapped round your neck like a scarf.

It would be even better if they were . . . things, Emily thought to herself, climbing out of bed and tugging the duvet with her like a squashy coat. Or animals. A sad little creature that you could cheer up with a saucer of milk, so you stopped being miserable, or worried.

She curled herself up with her duvet on her window seat and gazed into the strangely slanted glass. It was greenish and old, as old as the house, and it had been made by hand, her father said. If Emily looked hard enough at the swirls and tiny bubbles, usually something would appear, although she never knew what it would be, or whether she would like it.

A few weeks before, when Emily had started to feel that she was different, the visions in the windows had seemed just another proof that there was something wrong with her. She had tried not to see them, and she'd moved her chair to the other side of the table, facing away from the glass. But she had missed the pictures.

Emily had always loved them, right from when the funny little room in the tower had first been hers, when she was five and old enough to walk up the steep, narrow staircase without falling. She adored her room. She could sit for hours drawing the strange things she saw in the window – cities made of clouds, strange creatures dancing through rivers of light. Now she knew that her pictures were probably real somewhere. And that all along the fairy world had been trying to entice her in.

Emily leaned her cheek against the cool green glass and looked at it out of the corner of her eye, hoping to catch a hint of movement.

A faint misty swirl, far off inside the glass, darkened and seemed to come towards her, becoming clearer and more solid as it paced slowly forward. A small, dark grey bear padded into view, its head hanging down, and Emily swallowed. It was exactly how she felt.

The bear sat down, just on the other side of the glass from Emily, and leaned forward, as though to place its damp black nose on her shoulder, or in the crease at the top of her neck. Emily could almost feel him through the glass, and she shivered with excitement. She'd never been able to touch the pictures in the glass before. She was sure her dad was right – now that she had been through the doors, there was magic inside her too. . .

The bear sighed mournfully, and Emily giggled. She could feel its sad breath and tickly whiskers on her ear. "I don't know how you did it, or if you even meant to, but I do feel a bit better."

"Do you want anything particular in your lunch?" Eva, Emily's mother asked, waving a buttery knife at her. "Do you think you ought to take two drinks? You'll probably boil shut up in a coach today; it's going to be really hot again."

Emily gaped at her. She was feeling a lot better than she had when she'd first woken up – seeing her unhappiness as a small grey bear really had taken the worst out of it. But she had a horrible feeling that as soon as she saw Katie, that awful fog of silence was going to wrap itself around her again.

Lory rolled her eyes. "Emily, you look like a fish."

Emily closed her mouth, and her mother came over to the table and looked at her worriedly. "Are you all right?" Then she frowned. "Emily, you haven't been – travelling?"

Eva meant dreaming her way through the doors, Emily knew. She had done it before, without meaning to, and without understanding that it was anything more than a strange and very real sort of dream. She had found herself on a riverbank, talking to the water-fairy girl from the mirror.

"No." Emily shook her head. "But I never tried to," she added honestly. "When it happened before, it just happened, so I don't know how I stop it happening again."

Eva licked thoughtfully at the butter on the knife, her tongue pink and pointed, like a cat's. "True. You're quite right, we should have thought of that. Remind me, darling, when you get home, and we'll ward your room." Then she shook herself. "And what I was trying to say, Ems, is that it's your school trip, so do you want anything different in your lunch?" She smiled, making herself suddenly far more fairy-like. Her smile stretched wide across her face, showing a mouthful of shining teeth. "Had you really forgotten?"

"Yes," Emily admitted. She supposed that Mrs Daunt had spoken about the trip yesterday at school, but she'd hardly been listening.

Now she stared down at her plate, frowning worriedly. She was going to have to talk to Rachel – she had to tell her *something*. She couldn't spend an hour or so sitting next to her best friend on a coach without saying anything to her. Emily sighed. Obviously it would be impossible to tell Rachel the whole truth – but a bit of it would surely be all right?

"Mum. . ."

"Mmm?" Her mother turned round from

cramming an extra juice carton into Emily's lunch box.

"Can I tell Rachel anything about . . . well, you know."

Her mother stared at her. "No. No, most definitely not. I'm sorry, Emily."

Emily watched unhappily as her mother's hand crept up, as though it wanted to point at her. As though her mother was considering a spell for silence. She had done it to Robin, after all – he'd told Emily so.

"All right, I won't," she said hurriedly, and the tautness went out of her mother's spread fingers.

"I'm sorry, Ems. But we just can't risk it. You do understand?"

Emily nodded. She did understand. It was just

71

that she wanted to talk to someone without wings about it. "Can't I at least say that I found out I'm adopted?" she pleaded. "I won't say anything, you know . . . that's really secret. . ."

Eva sighed. "I suppose so."

"Are you coming?" Robin asked Emily impatiently. He liked to get to school early to play football, which he was very good at. He was unfairly fast and he had amazing reflexes. It was no wonder his side almost always won.

"Are we meeting Rachel?" he asked, glancing up at her as they went out of the front door.

"Yes!" Emily said, a little sharply. "Why wouldn't we be?"

"Don't snap at *me* just because you've had a fight with her!" Robin said, in a sing-song voice.

72

Emily folded her bottom lip in and bit it, to stop herself losing her temper. "It wasn't really a fight," she muttered. And it would be a great pleasure to tell Rachel exactly what Robin was, and leave him to deal with it.

She smiled to herself, and then waved at Rachel, who was just coming round the corner looking unsure. Emily waved far more happily than she would have done without Robin irritating her, and she caught a quick delighted smile dart across Rachel's face.

Robin hurried off ahead of them, leaving Emily and Rachel walking slowly side by side, occasionally glancing at each other.

"I'm sorry," Emily murmured as they came to the end of her road.

"What for?" Rachel asked uncomfortably.

"Not telling you this before. . ." Emily sighed and looked behind her. She didn't want anyone else hearing what she was about to say. "You were right when you said I'd never have been upset by Katie like that, until yesterday. She never worried me all that much before – I mean, she says horrible things, but she can't really do anything, can she?"

I knew who I was before, she realized. *I really belonged. Katie couldn't take that away from me, whatever she said. It was like standing on a good solid floor. And now I've got a wobbly branch or something instead.* She swallowed, and stuffed her hands in the pockets of her school dress. "I found out I was adopted."

Rachel stopped walking and stared at Emily, her mouth open.

"Are you . . . no, you mean it. . . Your mum and dad aren't really your parents?"

Emily shook her hair so it hid her face. "They adopted me when I was a baby."

"When? I mean, when did they tell you?" Rachel whispered.

"Last weekend."

"And you never knew before? Your mum and dad never said anything?"

Emily sighed and shrugged. "No. But things were feeling weird. I knew something was going on." She glanced up apologetically at Rachel. "I even wondered if they might be splitting up."

Rachel snorted. "I don't think so. Well, I

suppose you never know, but your parents are always nice to each other. Not just polite nice. I mean you can tell they really like each other."

"Mmm. But it was all I could think of. There were all these odd moments – like someone wanted to say something and couldn't quite do it." Emily shivered, remembering the oddness and all the other things that had happened, the ones she definitely couldn't tell Rachel. "Then we had a big family dinner together on Saturday night." She gave a strange little gasp, remembering the dryness of the roast chicken in her mouth, the way she could hardly swallow. "That's when they told me," she went on, her voice very high and thin. It was harder to talk about it than she'd thought it would be.

"I'm sorry I was cross with you yesterday." Rachel looked at her anxiously. "I shouldn't have had a go at you. And then I was all sulky. You shouldn't *have* to tell me stuff. I mean – that's a huge thing. I can see why you didn't want to talk about it now. I just didn't know. . ." She trailed off. "I really am sorry."

"Oh shut up saying sorry!" Emily hugged her.

"Lark and Lory and Robin aren't adopted too?" Rachel said suddenly, as they set off walking again.

Emily shook her head. "No. Which makes it worse. I'm the odd one out. I don't belong and they do."

Rachel frowned. "I suppose. . . I mean, yes, not by blood. . . But do you really feel like that?

That you aren't part of them? It never seemed like you were any different. Not the way your mum and dad treated you all."

"I know." Emily kicked at a leaf on the pavement and sighed. "I think that's making it worse, though. If I didn't like being Emily Feather, and I didn't love them, I wouldn't mind, would I? I'd be glad that I'd got another family somewhere. My real family. But I'm not glad at all. I just want to be me." She sniffed, refusing to cry again. "That's why it was so hard when Katie said those things. I *am* weird. I don't know who *me* is any more."

Rachel made a noise Emily had never heard her make before. A sort of furious growl. It was so surprising that Emily giggled – it was like hearing a rabbit roar.

"She'd better not do it again," Rachel snarled. "And if she says you smell, there's a simple answer, isn't there?" She put her arm round Emily's shoulders. "We can just tell Katie to put a bag over her head. That'll be an improvement for everybody."

Emily yawned and blinked as Rachel nudged her. She'd almost been asleep.

"We're nearly there. Wake up, Emily, Mrs Daunt's doing her how-we-expect-you-to-behave-not-like-when-you-went-to-the-farm-last-year talk. She definitely doesn't expect people sleeping while she's moaning."

"Wasn't asleep," Emily murmured, but the

coach was pulling into a car park, and wasn't on the motorway any more. She blinked stickiness out of her eyes and tried to concentrate. This trip to the city gallery was to do with their literacy topic, writing in response to stimulus — which just meant seeing something and writing a story about it. They were supposed to choose pictures that they liked and write a story inspired by them. Emily suspected that she wasn't going to enjoy it. And she had a feeling that whichever painting she chose, strange details were going to creep into her story. Some things she'd seen over the last fortnight were engraved deeply in her memory — Lark and Lory unfurling their glorious, bird-like wings. Her mother's huge, glowing eyes. Robin's flaming hair and translucent skin. The strange otherness of her father's face, once he'd let her see his real self.

How could she make anything up when all that was filling her head? She could write down what was really happening to her right now, and Mrs Daunt would probably tell her not to let her imagination run away with her.

Thankfully, the gallery was beautifully cool. Emily let out a sigh of pleasure as they stepped through the glass doors and into the light, open rooms.

"This place is huge," Rachel murmured, sounding awed, and a bit worried. "How are we supposed to choose just one painting? There must be thousands."

"At least," Emily agreed, looking at the little map that had been handed out, and then peering ahead through the gallery and seeing the rooms opening out in front of them like a maze. "But Mrs Daunt said we had to stick to just this floor. So that cuts it down to maybe only a few hundred to look at?" She smiled, the delicious open whiteness of the gallery, studded with jewel-like paintings, had already lifted her out of her gloom.

Emily had been to galleries before – her mother went all the time, and she would have liked to take them all with her, but Lark and Lory and Robin always moaned. Eva had told Emily that she loved bringing her to see new exhibitions. It was their special time together.

Often they'd go home afterwards and sit in Eva's studio, drinking hot chocolate and drawing. Eva would scribble designs for beautiful new clothes in page after page of a sketch pad, and Emily would lie on the floor underneath her mother's cutting table, covering huge pieces of paper with coloured pencils or sweeps of pastel chalk.

Eva said she loved it that at least one of her children shared her passion for art. Emily blinked slowly. She could hear her mother saying it now, after Robin had told her he'd rather eat worms than go to another art gallery. *At least one of my children*. . . It had never sounded forced. Emily shivered a little, with a sort of relieved happiness. She did belong in some ways. Of course, she hadn't really inherited her love of drawing from Eva, but she'd spent hours and hours borrowing pencils and bits of paper while her mother worked. She remembered being tiny and trying to copy the colours of the fabrics that Eva was cutting and twisting. It had grown into her. Surely that counted too?

Emily nodded to herself. If Eva were here, she'd say to ignore Mrs Daunt's questions and walk round the paintings until Emily found one that spoke to her. Emily thought she was right, but she didn't want to get into trouble for not doing the quiz. If she and Rachel did it together quickly, then they could go for a proper explore. She tapped her pencil against the clipboard and looked at the first question. "We're in the wrong room, I think."

The quiz took them all round the gallery, and by the time they'd finished it – counting numbers of children in strange family groups, and naming horses, and spotting snails in still lives – even Emily was almost sick of paintings.

"Done!" Rachel said gleefully, scribbling in the final answer, and they collapsed on to one of the low wooden benches. "It has to be time for lunch?" she added hopefully.

"No." Emily checked her watch and sighed. "No, we've got at least another hour before we have to meet up for lunch. We're having it late, remember, just before we get back on the coach. Do you want to go and look for a painting for your story?"

"No. But I suppose we ought to." Rachel heaved herself up from the bench reluctantly. "Did you see anything you want to write about?"

Emily shook her head slowly, but she wasn't listening. Something had caught her — she was hooked, it felt like. As though something was calling to the tiny fraction of magic that had buried itself inside her. It pulled her in. She glanced around eagerly, trying to see what it was.

A streak of colour was shining at her from the next room – no, not even the next one, but the one beyond that. It was a fragment of shining blue, a colour that made Emily think of butterflies' wings.

She smiled. Now she could see them, fluttering

87

around the skylight above her head, circling and darting, and then tempting her on through the doorway to the rooms ahead.

Emily grabbed Rachel's wrist and pulled her. "This way," she murmured, forgetting that she was tired and hungry and sick of paintings. She wanted desperately to find that patch of blue, and feast on it.

The painting was of a girl, standing in the shadows of a stone building – a broken tower, or perhaps just a garden summerhouse. She was looking sideways, and Emily couldn't tell if she was meant to be hiding – there was a hint of a smile at the corner of her mouth, as if she thought she had found the perfect place – or if she was waiting for someone to meet her. Emily just wished that the girl would look up. She wanted to gaze into her eyes. She was almost sure that there would be a message in them for her.

It was the girl's dress that was the calling blue, and as Emily stood gazing in front of the painting, still gripping Rachel's wrist, the butterflies shimmered and settled back into the silken folds, making the skirt ripple, as though a light wind had blown through the garden.

"It's so *real*," Rachel whispered.

Emily shook herself, and took a sharp breath in. She hadn't breathed since her first glimpse of that amazing blue, she realized. "I know. It's wonderful. . ." The butterflies had gone, and the dress was only paint again. Emily longed to stroke it, to see if she could feel the silk, or the dusty softness of wings, but she knew the magic wasn't there. It wasn't the painted girl who had been calling, Emily felt sure. She could feel the magic still pulling at her from another corner of the room. Something else had stolen the blue from the girl's skirt and sent the butterflies out to call Emily. It was close, though. The air was quivering with power, a feeling that Emily remembered from her dreams. Something needed her.

"Emily, are you going to choose this one for your story?" Rachel asked her hopefully.

Emily stared at her, forgetting for a moment what they were supposed to be doing. "Oh! No. No, I think I'll look for something else," she murmured. Her fingertips itched with the need to find where the magic was coming from.

"Oh, good, because if you really don't want it, then I'll have it!" Rachel said gratefully, sitting down on the floor in front of the painting and staring at it lovingly.

Perhaps there *was* still some magic in it? Emily wondered, looking at her in surprise. The painting seemed to have enchanted Rachel. The hiding girl smiled sweetly at the crushed petals by her feet, and Emily shuddered. She must make sure to pull her friend away from that painting when she went for lunch. Rachel looked as though she could stare at it for years, her eyes darting busily between the girl and the story she was already scribbling. There was a wisp of power buried somehow in those swirls of silk, and it had wrapped itself round Rachel.

Emily began to walk slowly around the room, glancing back occasionally to check that Rachel was all right. After her father's warnings, Emily was more worried about magic outside the house, when she was nowhere near any of her family. She wasn't sure who she could trust. But the girl hadn't moved again – perhaps it was just the beauty of the painting that was holding Rachel so close.

The colours in this room seemed especially bright, and Emily stared at them hungrily. The paintings were like jewels; some of them even had golden frames painted round them, like necklaces. But they reminded Emily of those enchanted fruits too, the ones that Lark and Lory had stopped her eating. Perhaps the paintings were bespelled somehow? Her father had said there were other doors. . . Emily wondered if he had ever visited this gallery.

Emily dug her fingernails into her palms, telling herself to be wary. If there was a door here, she mustn't be tempted in – she had promised Ash and Eva she would not go on her own.

At last she stopped in front of a painting that was lurking in the corner of the gallery. There were several other people in the room, but they had all passed it by with a vague glance – it seemed busy and muddy-coloured. But Emily was sure that there was something more – she could feel the power in the dull canvas. She stepped closer, her hand creeping up to cover her mouth in amazement.

It was moving. Hundreds of tiny figures fought and talked and shopped and wrangled in a landscape of tree-sized daisies and chestnuts that looked like boulders. Emily glanced behind her, suddenly worried that this was desperately secret, and that she mustn't let anyone else see what was happening. Then she noticed the label on the wall beside the painting – a label just like those on all the other paintings around the gallery. This painting had been here for years, and for years people had walked past it without seeing what it was. Emily reached out one finger and cautiously stroked the frame, trying to feel the magic.

As she touched the gilded wood of the frame,

the painting suddenly sprang into full colour, as though only a washed-out, greyish version lived in the gallery from day to day. The faint flickers and shifts of movement that Emily had seen before turned to dancing life, and the noise swelled out of the frame. A shrieking gang of fairy children chased each other in and out of daisies and twining columbine, and a plump young girl with ragged butterfly wings stared out at Emily in amazement, nudging her friend and pointing. Then the pair of them dissolved into giggles, as though Emily was the funniest thing they had ever seen, and fluttered away into the tall grass stems that framed the main scene, peeping back every so often and sniggering behind their hands.

Emily sighed. She had hoped to ask one of the

fairies from the painting how it was that she could see them, and whether the painting was another door into their world from hers. But there was clearly no point asking those two anything. They reminded her of Lara and Ellie-Mae.

Still – here was a chance to answer some of those questions that she kept forgetting to write down. At one point during last week's history lesson, Emily had looked thoughtfully at a picture of a Roman general on a horse, and wondered if centaurs were real. And now a dark centaur archer was glaring at her out of the painting.

Emily practically pressed her nose up against the canvas, trying to see all the detail that she could. She wondered what the art gallery looked like to the fairy people on the other side – was it just a little window? A hole in the sky? And did she look her own size, or smaller? It was impossible to tell.

"Please. . ."

It was the merest whisper, so soft that Emily hardly heard it. She stepped back from the painting, frowning and trying to see which of the hundreds of tiny creatures had spoken – she was almost sure that whoever it was had been speaking to her; had recognized the magic inside her and called her from across the gallery.

"Help me. . ."

Emily scanned the painting desperately, her stomach twisting. There was such fear in that tiny voice. No one inside the painting seemed to have heard – but a tiny creature at the far side of the canvas was peering out at her now, looking over the edge of a rocky crag and beckoning to her. "Help me!" she whispered again, her pale little face twisting with fright.

"I can't come in," Emily whispered. "I don't know how – I can only see. And I'm not allowed. . . They said it was dangerous. . ."

It seemed a very feeble set of excuses, and the girl's shoulders drooped. She looked behind her anxiously, and then she sprang up, scrambling her way on to the top of the jutting cliff and darting in and out of the other creatures, always looking behind her, as though she expected to see something dreadful come clambering over the cliff edge after her. Each time the girl glanced back, her hair swung wildly around her head. It swirled like weeds in a fast-flowing river and waved around her pale face. The long fingers that had stretched out and caught desperately at the handholds in the rock as she climbed, were webbed, and Emily let out a little gasp of recognition.

It was the girl from the mirror.

Emily watched, her heart thudding in her chest as she wondered what was chasing the girl. She stared at the grasses waving gently along the rocky edge where the girl had climbed into view, waiting for huge claws to gouge their way up the stone. Or if not a monster, then a gang of huntsmen, like those who had chased her and her sisters. It was the thought of those huntsmen that made her try to reach into the painting. She had promised not to, but this was different. How could she watch the green-haired girl run, scared as she was, and *not* help her?

She stretched out her hand, brushing her fingertips against the canvas. It was the strangest feeling – there was paint there under her fingers, but at the same time she could feel that she was reaching out beyond the painting and into something far away.

Until someone caught her arm and pulled her sharply back. The figures in the painting were suddenly dull and grey and still, and she looked up to see an angry man in a dark uniform glaring down at her.

5

The security guard pulled her away from the painting, glowering at her. "Where's your teacher?" he snapped.

"I – I don't know," Emily stammered. She felt dizzy, and not anchored to the ground. She wondered vaguely if she'd left part of herself inside the strange world of the painting when she was dragged back so suddenly. She certainly didn't feel all there. She noticed Rachel hovering worriedly at the security guard's elbow, and a couple of other people from their class whispering to each other in the doorway. As her vision cleared, she saw that it was Katie and Ellie-Mae – of course it was. Emily gave a tiny sigh, and then stared down at her feet as Mrs Daunt hurried into the gallery. She seemed to arrive out of nowhere, as though she'd suddenly sensed that one of her group was causing trouble.

"There are strict guidelines," the security guard was telling her, and Mrs Daunt alternated between nodding apologetically to him and glaring at Emily.

Emily decided she'd better start thinking of

an excuse quite quickly. No one was going to believe that she was trying to rescue a fairy girl in a painting. She glanced back at it, hoping that the river fairy was still there, and hadn't been eaten, or shot down with arrows.

The painting wasn't even moving for Emily now. It was greyly, eerily still. All the little figures were fixed, their faces frozen. Emily longed to reach out and touch the paint again – they looked so wrong, so *silly* like that. She knew that they were real, and it hurt to see them reduced to a strange, rather pretty picture. And then she saw, with a lurch deep in her stomach, that there were figures, now, at the bottom of the cliff, staring up at the girl

"Well? What on earth were you doing, Emily?

You know not to touch the paintings!" Mrs Daunt snapped. "Look at me!"

Emily swallowed, and dragged herself away from the girl's frightened face. "I'm really sorry! I was looking at it, and then I saw a fly land on the painting –" there were several small black flies in the gallery, lazily circling in the warmer air under the skylight "– so I brushed it off. It's such a beautiful painting, I didn't think properly. I just didn't want it to have a fly on it. . ."

Not a brilliant excuse, she realized, crossing her fingers behind her back, but the best she could manage right now.

"You didn't think properly. Exactly," Mrs Daunt told her. But she seemed slightly less furious than she'd been before. "I'm so sorry," she said again to the guard. "I think it *was* a silly mistake. I'm sure she didn't intend to damage the painting." Mrs Daunt turned to look at it properly for the first time, and frowned. "Are you using this one for your project, Emily?"

"Um, yes. . ." Emily answered. She hadn't found another painting, so she supposed she'd have to. She could write something about how horrible those girls who reminded her of Lara and Ellie-Mae were, she supposed. There was no way she was going to turn the hunt into a story. She looked back at the painting worriedly, but it still hadn't moved. The girl was stretched spider-like across the top of the rock, staring down behind her with terrified eyes. It was as if time had stopped there, inside the painting. Crossing her fingers behind her, Emily hoped desperately that it had. Perhaps the fairy girl would be safe until someone else looked at the painting, *really* looked at it? Someone who understood what it was.

How many people like that could there be? Emily wondered, as Mrs Daunt marched her away towards the room where they were having lunch. As they disappeared through the doorway, she glanced back one more time, but the painting was faded and muddy again, in the corner of the gallery.

"A fly? Really?" Rachel whispered, as Mrs Daunt turned away to talk to one of the other teachers.

Emily nodded. "I just didn't think. . ." she repeated.

106

Rachel looked at her doubtfully. "Why were you staring at that painting for such a long time, anyway? It was nothing special."

"I liked it," Emily said vaguely, shrugging. "It was interesting."

"Have you worked out what you're going to write? I've got some of mine done already," Rachel added, patting the cover of her notebook. "And Miss Gray says there are postcards of that painting in the shop, so I'll buy one. Maybe even a poster."

Emily smiled, trying to put the girl's frightened face out of her mind. She was almost sure there would be no postcards of her painting. "You really love it, don't you?"

Rachel nodded. "There's something odd about it – I almost feel like I can still see the blue

107

behind my eyes. I know that sounds stupid," she added hurriedly.

"It doesn't," Emily told her. In the fuss with the security guard, she had forgotten the butterflies that had called them into that particular room. They had been sent on purpose to fetch her, she suspected. The river fairy had felt her coming, and known her, and called to her for help. The way she had helped Emily and her sisters only a few days before.

Emily pushed her half-eaten sandwich back into her bag and sighed.

She would just have to go back and get her.

"There's a horrible smell on this coach." The voice came floating over the back of the seat, quiet but clear, and Emily flinched, staring wide-eyed at Rachel. She hadn't noticed Katie sitting down behind them. But now she could hear Ellie-Mae laughing, and she could see her peeping between the two coach seats. Then Katie leaned round the side of the seat and smiled at Rachel.

"Can't you smell it?" she asked sweetly.

"No," Rachel snapped back. Then she glanced at Emily, looking shocked at herself. She never, ever talked back to Katie.

Katie seemed surprised too. A reddish flush darkened across the tops of her cheeks, and she stopped smiling. "Only someone as sad as you would be friends with her."

Rachel closed her eyes for a moment, as though she was nerving herself to do something crazy and dangerous, like jumping off a cliff. "I could say the same to you," she said, gabbling it quite fast.

"What did she say?" Ellie-Mae asked indignantly after a moment. "Does she mean me?"

"Yes." Rachel actually crossed her fingers this time, Emily noticed. "You're welcome to each other. No one else likes you. Oh, except Lara, and that says a lot, doesn't it?"

"Rachel!" Emily whispered, forgetting about the river-girl in the gallery she was so shocked. She wrapped her hand round her friend's crossed fingers. Rachel had talked brave that morning, but Emily had never expected her to actually stand up to Katie and her friends.

"No one likes you either," Katie said furiously.

"Brilliant comeback. . ." Rachel said in a scornful voice, gripping Emily's hand. She'd actually gone white, and Emily really hoped she wasn't going to be sick.

Some of the other girls in their class were watching now, the ones sitting on the other side of the aisle and in front of Rachel and Emily. Their little bit of the coach had gone very, very quiet.

Emily was sure that Katie had noticed this too. She moved so that she was looking over the back of her seat instead, and she stared down at Rachel. They looked just as pale as each other.

"I could spit on you from here." Katie hissed.

"Only stupid people who can't think what

111

to say spit," Rachel said disgustedly, but she twitched as though she was scared that Katie would do it.

"You spit at her and I'll tell," Emily hissed, deciding that now was the time to join in.

"Oh, little smelly Emily's going to tell," sing-songed Katie. "Would that be Mrs Daunt you were telling, Emily? Because I don't think you're her favourite person right now, you know. Not since you starting vandalizing valuable paintings."

"I didn't." Emily rolled her eyes.

Katie shrugged. "Maybe. It looked like you did. And if you tell Mrs Daunt anything, I'll tell her I saw you get out a pen, and you were just about to write on that painting, except you got caught first. Who's she going to believe?"

"Emily," Rachel said flatly. "You've been caught bullying people before. Mrs Daunt knows what you're like. Stupid, and mean."

There was a sharp indrawn breath from the girls sitting around them, and even people sitting further away were leaning round to see what was going on now. Emily swallowed worriedly. Katie had a reputation to keep up. If Rachel kept taunting her, Katie would have to do something incredibly horrible to keep everyone scared of her.

Katie obviously decided exactly the same thing. Her dark eyes hardened, and developed a glassy sheen like black marbles. Then she darted out one plump white hand and wound it swiftly into Emily's hair – Emily's, not Rachel's,

113

as though she knew who was to blame for this strange rebellion. She jerked her hand back, yanking at Emily's hair so hard that she yelped and her eyes filled with tears.

Everyone gasped, and most of the girls around them pretended not to be looking. Katie sat back with a hank of Emily's hair still wrapped round her hand. She smiled triumphantly at Emily, who was clutching the side of her head and still gasping.

"She pulled your hair out!" Rachel whispered, horrified.

"I know," Emily agreed, grimacing as she rubbed her hand across her eyes. "I can feel it."

"Still want to tell?" Katie murmured through the gap between the seats.

114

Emily didn't say anything – for once, she couldn't think of anything to say.

"What's the matter?" Robin stared at Emily, frowning.

"Nothing." Emily walked on down the road.

"No, there is; you look funny."

Emily glanced round at him in surprise. Rachel had lent her a hair band and she'd pulled her hair back in a loose sort of knot. She'd checked in the loos before they left school – she definitely couldn't see the tiny bare patch. She was sure Robin couldn't either. "I don't. . ." she said doubtfully.

Robin flicked a glance under his eyelashes at Rachel and muttered, "I'll talk to you at home."

115

He couldn't say what he wanted to say in front of Rachel, Emily realized. It probably meant that he wasn't looking at her in the way anyone else would. Perhaps it was the same sort of thing as the miserable fog feeling he'd sensed around the girls the day before. He could sense what had happened to her. Or at least that something had.

"You don't want to tell him?" Rachel whispered as Robin stalked away in front of them.

"He'd probably tell my mum." Emily shrugged. "I just don't feel like turning it into a big drama. She'd be up at the school in minutes, having a go at Mrs Daunt. My life wouldn't be worth living."

"I suppose," Rachel said doubtfully. "But

maybe someone should tell the school. She pulled out a chunk of your hair!"

"I'll make her stop somehow," Emily said wearily. "I don't want to bring my parents into it, that's all." She frowned, imagining what her mum could do to Katie if she felt like it. She wouldn't use magic, of course, she was far too sensible. But she might be *tempted* to. And Emily didn't want her to be upset.

Emily shook her head firmly. It didn't hurt that much now. No real harm done, she told herself.

Providing Katie wasn't actually a witch. If she was, what might she do with a lock of Emily's hair?

Emily shuddered, imagining cruel spells – perhaps one of those wax dolls with pins stuck in. She fluttered her fingers cautiously and glanced down at her feet as she walked on. No bits of her hurt yet. . . Then she shrugged crossly. She was worrying herself for nothing. Katie was truly horrible, but being able to spot people's weaknesses didn't make her a witch. There was no magical excuse for any of this. Katie was only normally nasty. Emily and Rachel had to not let her get to them, that was all.

And I won't, Emily said to herself firmly, snatching back the hand that was fingering the torn spot on her scalp. *I just need to work out how.*

"You'll be all right?" Rachel said to her anxiously as they came up to the house gate, where Robin was waiting, hopping from foot to foot impatiently.

"Fine," Emily gave her a tiny smile.

Rachel nodded. She looked very determined, though still a bit white around the mouth. "We won't let her keep doing this sort of stuff, I promise."

"Come on." Robin glared at Emily, and she shifted her school bag on her shoulder uneasily. He could tell she was hiding something, and he wanted to know.

"Bye!" she called to Rachel, and hurried up the path, hunting for her key, with Robin trotting behind her. The mermaid door knocker on the front door flicked its tail, and then the brassy little face twisted and peered down at her curiously. Maybe it wasn't only Robin who could sense what had been happening. Her parents had strengthened the door spells after Emily accidentally blundered through, so she supposed it was like an extra-sensitive burglar alarm now. The whole house was guarding her. Emily wasn't quite sure how she felt about that.

"Ssshhh!" Robin hissed at her, shutting the front door very quietly.

"What?" Emily blinked at him, surprised, and he pulled her up the stairs after him. He stopped when they were round the turn in the stairs, and sat down, staring at her determinedly.

"What happened?"

"I don't know what you mean," Emily murmured, but she glanced away from him. His dark blue eyes were suddenly so water-like that they seemed to swirl and ripple, and she would have told him anything if she had looked at him much longer.

"You shouldn't be able to do that," Robin said crossly. "I was trying to spell you, and you broke away! You've lived with us for too long, that's what it is. You're too used to magic."

"Really?" Emily asked him, feeling rather pleased. When she'd first begun to see the odd things in the house, she'd wondered if maybe she had some strange sort of powers. It had been a terrible disappointment when she found out that actually, she was the only one of them who didn't. So it was good to know that at least the little scrap of magic that had grown inside her was useful for *something*.

"Really. It must be because you've been around me and Lark and Lory so much. You've got an immunity. Because when I looked at you like that you should have been completely hypnotized, and told me *exactly what's been going on*!"

Emily sighed, and decided that Robin wasn't going to leave her alone. She'd have to tell him — after all, if she didn't, he'd just go and find out about it from someone at school.

"Katie Meadows was teasing me, that's all. You know what she's like."

Robin blinked thoughtfully. "Oh. That girl who looks a bit like a slug?"

"Does she?" Emily frowned. "I don't think so."

"To me she does. She's slimy. What did she do?"

Emily was silent for two seconds too long. "She was just mean," she said unconvincingly.

"And?" Robin hugged her, and then he whispered sweetly in her ear, much more sweetly than he ever usually spoke to her. "I can make you tell me, you know."

"Oh, all right!" Emily snapped. "If you must know, she pulled my hair."

Robin didn't look convinced. "I pull your hair, Emily, all the time. What did she really do?"

"You don't pull chunks of it *out*."

Robin sucked in a breath through his teeth and stroked his thin fingers across the side of her hair. Emily could feel each separate hair tingling with his magic, and she was sure that when she next looked in a mirror, her hair would be about

123

three times more curly than usual. But probably nice and shiny too.

"I'll make all her hair fall out," Robin snarled as he came across the raw patch, and Emily flinched. "How *dare* she?" There was a sudden warmth all through the roots of Emily's hair, and the dull ache of the torn patch disappeared.

"Thanks!" Emily explored it carefully with her fingertips, but now it was just a patch of soft new skin.

"I can't make the hair grow back all at once," Robin said. He sounded rather annoyed about it. "Mum could, but I'm not strong enough."

"Don't tell her!"

Robin rolled his eyes. "I wasn't going to." Then he smiled. The smile made his eyes sparkle, but

Emily shivered. It was an icy sort of glint, and he looked furious, even with the smile. "I may not be able to make your hair grow, but I can deal with the rest of it quite well by myself."

"What do you mean?" Emily asked suspiciously. "You don't need to deal with anything. It's nothing to do with you!"

Robin shook his hair back, and Emily could see the pointed tips of his ears, and the unnatural whiteness of his teeth. "You're my sister. It's up to me to protect you."

Emily gave a little snort of laughter at the thought of her eight-year-old brother protecting her. But the tightness that had been knotting up inside her chest seemed to ease a little more every time Robin said something like this.

125

"Since when do you need to protect me?" she demanded. "You don't go round protecting Lark and Lory, do you?"

Robin shrugged. "You can't fly away. No slug gets to hurt my sister." He frowned and ran a finger round one of Emily's curls. "What shall we do to the slug?" Then he looked round at her excitedly. "Oh, we could turn her into one for real!"

"No!" Emily squeaked. "We can't! Not even Katie Meadows deserves to be a slug."

"Not for ever. . ." Robin suggested pleadingly. "Only for a day, maybe."

"How are we supposed to explain that she's disappeared?" Emily shook her head violently. "Honestly, Robin, you can't."

Robin looked at her suspiciously. "Are you just going to let her get away with it? You do that with me and Lark and Lory all the time, you know. You're such a wuss."

Emily stood up. "You put spells on me!" she snapped. "I can hardly do that back, can I? What do you expect?"

Robin shrugged. "You're just too nice. Look, can I at least put a slug in Katie's sandwiches? Not even by magic? I'll just catch one in the garden."

"No," Emily snapped, although the thought of Katie Meadows chewing a slug was very, very tempting. "You can't. I'll sort it out! I'll do something. I just haven't worked out what yet."

But as she hurried upstairs, she glanced back and caught Robin smiling to himself – a thoughtful, planning sort of smile.

6

Emily was curled up on her window seat with her chin on her arms, scowling at the misty glass. Everything around her reminded her of the fairy world. She couldn't even walk past the mirror on the landing without feeling guilty.

What was she going to do about the fairy girl from the riverbank?

Emily shook her head, trying to clear it a

little. There were far too many things to worry about, what with Robin obviously planning to take some sort of revenge on Katie. But the girl was the most important. Emily could still see her white, frightened face, and the way her fingers had clung to the rock.

If she hadn't promised her parents, she would have gone down to the landing right now and tried to open the door inside the mirror. Emily had almost gone through it once, when that same river-fairy girl had beckoned her in. Except that now, of course, the guard spells on all the doors had been strengthened. Emily wasn't sure that she'd be able to open it but she had to go back somehow, and help. She would have wanted to, even if it didn't feel like paying back a debt.

There had been such fear in the girl's silvery-green eyes. She couldn't leave her there, being hunted.

But her dad had said she wasn't to go. The worlds don't mix, he'd said. In other words, stay out and don't interfere. It was no good asking him or Mum for help.

She glanced round. There were light footsteps on the stairs. Her mother, at a guess. And the tappity-tap of claws, so she had Gruff with her. Emily smoothed the hair over the tiny bare patch on her scalp and tried to look not in the slightest bit like she was planning a trip through a forbidden door.

Her mother opened her purple bedroom door and smiled at her. "Emily! You and Robin should

131

have come and told me you were back. I was working on a design for a scarf and I didn't see the time. I only knew you were home because Robin came and told me he wanted toast and he'd already eaten all the bread at breakfast."

"Oh, there are some chocolate muffins left, in the tin in the cupboard." Emily started to get up, but her mother sat down next to her on the window seat and pulled her back with an arm around her shoulders. Gruff sat down next to them and leaned lovingly on Eva. He adored her, and she loved him dearly, despite the dark hairs he left on all her fabric samples.

"Robin can find them himself. You know him, Emily, he's probably on his second muffin already. Just because Robin's hungry, it doesn't mean you have to go running to feed him! You let him push you around too much. They all do."

Emily gave a tiny shrug. It was true – but then, they were special, and she wasn't.

Her mother leaned down and grabbed her shoulders. "I *saw* you think that! Don't you dare!"

"I like cooking for all of you," Emily murmured.

"I know. But you need to stand up for yourself sometimes."

"I'm trying," Emily said, with a sigh. First Rachel, then Robin, now Eva. Everyone seemed to be ordering her to stand up, be strong, and not let people push her around. . .

"Good. Now, we have to ward your room, remember? To stop you travelling in your sleep."

"Oh. . ." Emily stared up at her mother in

133

dismay. She had completely forgotten what Eva had said at breakfast. She had been depending on her dreams to help her rescue the river fairy from the painting. She had travelled before, after all. And now she *needed* to. Surely it would happen again?

"Don't worry!" Eva stroked her cheek. "Oh, Emily, don't look like that. I didn't mean to scare you. I'm sure you're not likely to travel, not now we've strengthened the guard spells. But just in case, we should make sure."

Emily nodded slowly. "What do we have to do?"

Her mother looked around the room. "All you have to do is sit on your bed. And stop looking so worried!"

Emily managed a small smile, but she was thinking furiously. Was there any way she could defeat the spell? To leave a chink in its armour somehow? Even without the river girl's desperate need, Emily hated the thought of shutting herself away from that amazing, magical place. She couldn't help feeling that she belonged there too, just a little.

But there was nothing she could do. She settled herself on her bed, watching her mother cautiously. Gruff lay down on the floor with his huge chin on his paws. Emily eyed him. She knew he was watching her. He was a guard dog of some sort. Emily never dreamed her way to anywhere else when Gruff slept on her bed, she was almost sure.

"Not there, Gruff," her mother said gently, snapping her fingers and beckoning the dog away from the bed. "I don't want you mixed up in the spell."

Gruff dipped his massive head in what looked like a nod, and moved back to stare at Emily from by the table.

The magic seemed to flow into the room suddenly, as though a huge fire had burnt up in seconds, swallowing her mother so that her red hair glowed and spat like real flames. Instead of heat, though, the real, fairy version of her mother gave off a delicious sweet coolness.

Emily sighed as the soft breeze lifted her hair. She felt so sleepily peaceful. She curled herself down against her pillow, twitching the edge of her sheet in her fingers, and closed her eyes. She could see her mother as a dark, reddish shape on the other side of her eyelids, dancing and dipping as she wove the spell.

Faintly, Emily could remember that she had meant to resist, but the spell-sleep was so soft and inviting that she couldn't. She sank deeper and deeper, and only woke when something touched her cheek with a butterfly lightness.

Emily's eyelids fluttered open, and she saw that her mother was sitting next to her. She had kissed her awake.

And the spell was cast.

Emily lay in bed that night with her sketchbook propped up on her pillow. She was trying to draw the river girl from the painting, before she forgot what she looked like. It seemed so long since she had helped them to escape on the banks of the river. And now she might never see her again! Emily didn't even know her name.

What would happen if those huntsmen caught her?

But her drawing had none of the urgency and life from the painting in the gallery. It was just a girl with greenish hair.

Emily sighed. She was going to have to ask Robin or Lark or Lory. They were going to be furious. Lark and Lory had already had to rescue her once, and if the gallery attendant hadn't stopped her, Emily was almost sure she would have gone inside that painting – that the river girl's magic had recognized her, and called her to help. If she had touched the canvas for just a little longer, the magic would have pulled her in. Then she would have been in some other world, stuck with a band of fairy hunters. They might even have been the same ones that the Ladies had sent after her and Lark and Lory before.

It would have been so much easier if she could just dream her way back to the gallery (carefully making sure not to dream any security guards), and just grab the girl and run.

Even in Emily's not-very-good drawing, the girl looked miserable. However slowly time went in that painting, Emily suspected she could still feel. She might be shut up inside the painted version of her story for years, waiting for the hunters to catch her! Emily shut the sketchbook with a slam. She didn't *know*! Maybe the painting meant nothing at all – it didn't really make sense that everything stopped when no one was looking, did it? Perhaps they'd already caught her.

Emily let out a little whimper of fright and crept out of bed. She'd talk to Lark first, she decided. She was the person least likely to shout.

It was still almost light, a hot summer evening. Emily was sure Lark wouldn't be asleep. She was most likely to be awake and chatting to Lory, which was a pity, because Lory would be angry when Emily told them what had nearly happened. But there was nothing she could do about it. She padded across to the door, shivering a little in the eerie moonlight. It turned her room into something strange, so that for a moment she wondered if the spell had failed, and she had already been asleep, and dreamed herself to another place.

Then she stopped, seeing a pool of dark shadow under the moonlit window, by the seat. It was where Gruff had been sitting as her mother cast the spell. Where she had *moved* him, so that he wasn't caught up in it.

The spell wasn't fixed to Emily! It was fixed to the bed where her mother expected her to sleep, and dream. Emily looked at the cushions on the window seat, frowning to herself. Could it really be that simple?

She had a moment of guilt as she curled herself up on the cushions. Her mother had trusted her – they had never thought that Emily might purposely dream her way out of the house. But she shook it away.

Emily had never tried to dream before. It was surprisingly difficult. She dreamed almost every night, although she didn't usually remember what had happened in her dreams. Only glimpses of odd journeys or places.

In the weeks before she'd found out about her family, her dreams had been even stranger than usual. She had seen things that felt real, while she knew that they couldn't be. She understood now that she had been gradually slipping through the thin veil between home and the other world where her family truly belonged.

She wriggled herself back into the cushions that she'd piled up and tried to imagine herself into the painting. But that was all she was doing — imagining. She could open her eyes any time and still be in her room. It was useless. And the more she worried about the girl and the hunters, the more useless it got. Emily stared miserably into the black glass of the window, her eyes dry and itchy with tiredness. She was weary, but she just couldn't seem to let go and sleep. It was so late now that the night was thickly dark through the window, so dark that she could only make out the faint orange glow of the street lamp across the road. The dirty yellow light mixed with the shadows inside the glass, building great towers of darkness that piled up against the sky.

Emily blinked, and shivered, as she watched the lights travelling slowly around the battlements of the dark palace. It seemed just the sort of place that whoever sent out the huntsmen would live. There would be night-dark dogs with burning eyes, and teeth that shone in the blackness under the trees. . .

She was there. The smell of woods was all around her, and she could feel dry leaves under her bare feet.

The trees rustled and creaked as the dogs padded hungrily under them, and Emily drew herself behind a massive trunk, hoping that the huntsmen's hounds would never smell a dream-girl.

She should have been pleased that she had

managed to dream her way in after all, but she was too scared. She almost wished she was still awake. What happened if you got eaten in a dream?

One of the dogs came sniffing hungrily past her hiding place, and Emily held her breath. If she breathed out, she would scream. . . She could hear its hoarse panting getting closer and closer, and she dug her fingers into the tree bark and squeezed her eyes tightly shut. Should she run? Or stay stone still, and trust to it only being a dream?

At last the dog seemed to give up, and she heard its paws padding heavily away through the bracken. Emily let out a shaky breath and started to edge slowly around the tree. She had to find out where she was. Had those dogs been hunting the girl? She suspected so – in which case she would need to follow them. She would have to try and get in front of them again. The thought made Emily feel sick, but she had to find her.

She inched her way carefully around the tree, pressing her fingers into the ridged bark. It seemed so safe here now, and the bark was almost friendly under her fingers. She hated to pull herself away. Reluctantly, she lifted her hand from the tree trunk – and touched something warm, something that flinched away from her in shock.

Emily stifled her scream, burying her knuckles in her mouth to muffle the noise.

"Who's there?" came a panicked whisper. A girl's voice – not a slavering hound. Unless the dogs could talk, of course. Emily gave a sharp gasp.

"Who are *you*?" she whispered.

"I asked first!"

It was true . . . she had. Emily swallowed. "I'm Emily. I came looking for someone." Someone, come to think of it, who was probably hiding, just like she was. . . She paused, and added doubtfully, "Is it you?"

The frightened person next to her in the dark was silent for a moment. Then she whispered, "You're the girl from the house?" There was a sudden hope in her voice.

"Yes!"

"I thought it was you. . . I felt you – just a scrap of magic, but it was close somehow. I didn't understand. Were you by the mirror?"

"No, I think it was another door. A secret door. One of those doors that aren't really allowed." Emily stumbled over the explanation. "It was in a painting. There was a gallery full of paintings, but I could feel you calling me out of one of them. I don't know how it ended up there. I suppose someone must have brought it back from your world."

"It's a very powerful spell, to make someone's picture," the girl whispered faintly. "I didn't think you'd come."

"I wanted to! I wanted to come before, but that man grabbed me. And then it was so hard to

148

get back. My parents made the spells stronger, you see, when they realized I'd gone through the doors. I promised I wouldn't do it again," she added hesitantly.

"You shouldn't have done," the girl agreed, and her voice sounded weary. "It's too dangerous. I shouldn't have called to you, but I was desperate, and I felt you close by. I'm sorry. . ."

"Of course you should have done!" Emily gripped the girl's cold hand. She could feel her shivering. "You helped us before; it was my turn. And I could tell how scared you were. I wanted to help *you*." She paused, suddenly feeling rather stupid. All she had been thinking was that she must get to the river girl and help her. She hadn't thought any further, and now both of them were

149

stuck in a dark wood, with hunters and dogs circling around them. She had no idea what to do next.

"You can't rescue me," the girl said gently. "I'm running from the Ladies' huntsmen."

"But we have to be able to do something," Emily whispered urgently. "Can't we find somewhere to hide? Until they've given up on you?"

"They won't give up! The hounds never give up on a quarry!"

Emily shook her head, confused. "But what are you going to do, then? You're worn out already. You can't just keep running for ever!"

"That's all there is. Better that than being chased down by the hounds."

Emily put her hand up against her mouth,

feeling suddenly sick. "They wouldn't . . . hurt you?"

"They would."

Emily took a deep, steadying breath and shook her head angrily. "No. And I don't care if it's against all the laws." She wrapped her arms tightly around the river-fairy girl and begged all the magic in the house to bring them home.

7

Emily was back on the window seat, shaking, and staring into the darkness. The cushions were still piled up around her as if she had never moved.

So it *had* been a dream – she had been here all the time. But surely she had brought the girl back out of the dream with her? She must have done. It couldn't all have been for nothing.

"Are you there?" she breathed, not daring to speak above a whisper. If it had worked, who was to say that the girl was all she had brought?

There was a waiting, anxious silence. And then someone shifted at the other end of the window seat, and the faintest shimmer of silver uncoiled itself and stood in front of her.

"Are we in one of the other places?" the river fairy asked, her voice breaking and squeaking a little. She sounded terrified.

"I'm sorry, I shouldn't have done it," Emily whispered. "I couldn't see what else to do. You were so frightened, and so tired. I didn't want them to catch you. Or me either," she added honestly. "I was dreaming, but it felt properly real. It felt like those hounds could have sniffed me out too." She reached out shyly to take the girl's hand again. "I'm so sorry."

But the river fairy knelt down in front of her, and her skin shone silvery in the dark, so that Emily could see she was smiling. She caught Emily's hands.

"I'm not angry. Please don't think that! You were right; I couldn't have run for much longer. It feels strange to be here –" she shivered a little "– but better here than thrown to the hounds."

"Uuurgh! They'd let the hounds eat. . . ? Oh no!" Emily pressed her hand to her mouth, disgusted.

"You really don't know?" The fairy girl stared

at her, and then smiled, seeming to find her innocence truly funny. "They only eat what they catch. That's why they're always hungry, and they never give up on a quarry."

Emily put both hands over her face now, her shoulders shaking. "How could they? And Ash and Eva come from there! My parents! They would never let anything like that happen."

The girl looked at her in surprise. "I suppose Lord Ash left to guard the ways before the Ladies began to grow so strong. The king stays shut away in the palace so much now – perhaps your parents don't know what it's like any more." She frowned. "But our world is a hard place. Cruel, sometimes."

Emily nodded. She'd had a glimpse of that,

155

when her father told her so firmly that the worlds must be kept apart. "What are we going to do?" she asked in a small, tired voice. "If I tell my family you're here, I don't think they'll be happy. No one is supposed to come through the doors without them knowing."

The girl glanced up at her. "They'll have seen us, then, the Lady Eva and Lord Ash." She looked round at the door anxiously, as though she expected someone to come storming through it, to send her back to the hounds.

Emily shook her head. "I don't think so. . . My mother made a spell, but it didn't work, because I cheated." She glanced down at her hands. "She laid it on my bed. It was to stop me dreaming – that's why I slept here by the window, and then

156

dreamed my way through the window glass to the woods, and you."

"You cheated one of *her* spells?" the girl asked, her eyes widening.

"I think so," Emily admitted. "Do you know her, my mother?"

"Of course. She's one of the great Ladies. There are stories about her. And Lord Ash is a prince – one of the king's highest courtiers."

"Really?" Emily blinked in surprise. Her dad spent most of his time shut up in his study under the stairs, typing and occasionally throwing things when work wasn't going as it should. He didn't seem princely at all. Although – she remembered his fairy form, the soft ash-grey of his skin and hair, the diamond blackness of his eyes. Perhaps he was.

"If you twisted your way out of her spell, there must be strong magic inside you," the girl said, squeezing Emily's hands. But it didn't make Emily feel much better.

"What are we going to do?" she asked again. When she'd set off on her daring rescue, she hadn't imagined bringing the girl back with her. She was just going to help, somehow, and that was all. . .

"You'll have to hide me," the river fairy murmured, looking around the room. "I'm not supposed to be here. There'll be trouble for everyone if I'm caught."

"Everyone?" Emily frowned. "Only me and you. It was me who brought you."

The girl sighed. "But who's going to believe that? You're a human child, you see. You aren't one of us, and you shouldn't have any magic. Lady Eva and the prince, that's who'll be blamed, if anyone finds out where I've gone. Or your sisters, perhaps."

Emily swallowed, suddenly seeing the truth of this. "You're right. Lark and Lory are already in trouble. Lots of trouble. My mum had to go and grovel, my father said." He'd explained it all to her only yesterday. It seemed an awfully long time ago. "It's because they came and dragged me away from the Ladies. . ." Emily leaned down and looked sharply at the river fairy. "Why were the huntsmen after you?"

The girl sighed, and her head drooped, the greenish-silver hair falling over her face. "They found out."

Emily's eyes widened, and she gripped the girl's hands tighter. "About you helping us escape? You mean you're in all this trouble because of *me*?"

The river girl didn't say anything, but Emily knew that it was true.

"Just because I got angry and ran through the doors by mistake. . ." Emily's voice shook.

"Yes."

Emily straightened her shoulders and tried to breathe, and think. "Will the huntsmen try and chase you here?" she asked, remembering the power and fearsomeness of Lady Anstis and the others. She couldn't imagine them giving up. "They shouldn't be allowed through the doors, but we did it, somehow. If we left traces, could they follow us?"

"I suppose they might," the girl agreed, glancing over her shoulder at the stormy glass in Emily's windows, and shuddering.

"But they don't know this place," Emily told her determinedly. "I'll hide you. We'll find somewhere, and we won't tell my parents either, in case they have to send you back." She shook her head. "I don't think they would. I don't see how they could be so cruel." But her dad had said, hadn't he? No mixing between the worlds. And her family had to live by the rules, Emily understood that. It didn't mean that she was going to let them give the girl back. "You hide for now – and then we'll find somewhere for you to go. To stay. . ." Her voice trailed away.

"Where can I hide?" the girl asked, looking around Emily's little room with a frown.

"What about the mirror on the landing?" Emily asked. "I saw you in it before. You were looking out at me, and I almost came through. Is it a mirror on your side too?" she asked curiously.

"No." The girl laughed. "Well, I was looking at it like a mirror. It was just a patch of sunlight on the water. It was glittering, and I looked in, and I saw you walking past. I could tell you were a human child. So I'd go back to look, in that same place. It didn't always work, but quite often I saw you, and I wondered who you were. Then one day you looked back."

Emily laughed. "You were the first fairy I saw.

Or the first one I knew about, anyway. Would another mirror work? Could you hide in it?"

"Maybe. But it would be better if there was some way you could keep me with you – if the huntsmen chase us down through your magic, I won't leave you to fight them on your own." She looked hopefully back at Emily. "Do you have any jewels?"

"Not really. I mean – bracelets and things. Is that what you mean?"

"Ye-es. Something small, that you can carry with you. I can work a spell to hide myself, I think. Especially if you help."

Emily nodded. "I know." She reached for her school bag, which was sitting on the table in front of the window seat, and rooted around in the inside pocket. "What about this?" It was a tiny mirror that Rachel had given her for Christmas, a round one set with sparkly jewels in the back.

"Yes." The fairy girl smiled, and came to sit next to Emily on the window seat, peering into the mirror. "Perfect. Hold it with me."

They cupped their hands together around the mirror, and Emily felt the rush of magic through the girl's fingers as she closed her eyes and began to whisper to herself. Something inside Emily seemed to jump, and a warmth spread through her, stretching out to the fairy by her side. Emily sighed delightedly as she saw her fingers glowing softly golden – and then she was holding the mirror by herself. The fairy girl had gone, and the mirror was dancing in her hands, the jewelled back tickling her fingers.

"Did it work?" she whispered hopefully. "Are you all right? Are you squashed?"

The fairy girl looked out at her from the mirror and laughed, and Emily laughed back. "I suppose not. I don't know how these things work."

"I shall be fine. But you should sleep. I'll watch, in case they come."

"What's that?" Robin demanded, looking over Emily's shoulder as she packed her things into her school bag and munched toast.

Emily jumped, and closed her hand over the glass. "Just a mirror."

Robin rolled his eyes. "If you're checking your hair, I can tell you now it's a total disaster at the back."

"Thanks," Emily muttered. She could feel the mirror quivering under her hand, as though the fairy girl was laughing.

"I'm going slug-hunting when I've finished my breakfast," Robin told her, grinning evilly, and Emily gave an anxious sigh.

"Don't you dare! I told you not to!" But Robin was gone. "He's as bad as Katie is," Emily growled to herself. He wasn't going to leave her alone about Katie, it was obvious. But she had more important things to worry about right now. Katie's nastiness didn't seem to matter much. Which actually meant it was a good day to laugh in Katie's face, if she got the chance.

Emily glanced over her shoulder. No one else around. She looked into the mirror again – it was full of swirling mist. She'd have to make sure it stayed hidden at school, or get the girl to make it look like a normal mirror somehow. She smiled to herself. She hoped the girl knew what a normal mirror was like. Probably all the ones she'd ever seen were haunted, or charmed, or had secret doors in them. She rubbed it gently and was about to call her when she frowned. She'd never asked. . .

"I've just thought of something," she whispered into the mist, and it cleared slowly to show the fairy girl's face.

"What is it?"

"I don't know your name. I'm sorry, I should have asked you. . . I've just been thinking of you as the river fairy."

"Oh." She smiled out of the glass and nodded. "Sasha. Like the sound of the water."

"It's pretty," Emily told her. "It suits you," she added shyly. "Look, I have to go to school, and we can't let anyone see you. I suppose I could hide the mirror in my pocket or something. But then you won't be able to see out. Can you make sure it stays looking like a mirror? Not misty, or anything like that?

She shuddered, imagining what would happen if Rachel happened to look in the mirror, or even worse, Katie or Ellie-Mae.

"What's the matter?" Sasha asked her curiously. "You look like someone walked over your grave."

Emily glanced at her, startled by the horrid phrase – and that Sasha could tell what she was feeling. "Oh... There are some girls teasing me. It's nothing. Nothing like you being chased. Don't worry about it."

"Why?" Sasha frowned at her out of the mirror, and Emily sighed.

"I don't think there's a reason. They're just like that."

"I can help." Sasha smiled, and Emily felt a sudden ripple of magic around her, soothing and gentle. "Don't be sad."

Emily sighed. "I'm not really. I was, but now I'm more worried about Robin. He wants to put

169

slugs in Katie's lunch – she's the worst of them. She pulled my hair out."

Sasha leaned closer to look at Emily properly, and the glass stretched and moulded so that her features jutted out of the mirror. Her voice was suddenly much more serious. "That's not just teasing."

Emily shrugged. "She does that sort of thing all the time," she murmured. "Not just to me."

"That's not right – there's someone coming!" Sasha sealed herself back into the glass in a second, and Emily scrabbled the mirror into her bag as Lark and Lory walked in.

"Aren't you ready for school?" Lark asked.

"Is she ever?" Lory flipped Emily's ponytail. "Hurry up."

170

Emily nodded, and grabbed the last, slightly stale chocolate-orange muffin out of the tin for breakfast on the way. She reckoned she might need it.

8

"Please tell me you didn't do it!" Emily whispered, sneaking in next to Robin in the lunch queue, and he shushed her crossly.

"Don't make it obvious!" he whispered. "Uh-huh. Two of them. She's got cheese and lettuce in her sandwich. It was perfect. It would have been harder to persuade the slugs in if it was ham or something."

Emily glanced sideways across the hall, looking for Katie.

"What's the matter?" Rachel asked, leaning over to look too. "You've gone pale."

"I feel sick. Robin put slugs in Katie Meadows' cheese sandwiches. We can't let her eat them!"

"Oh no," Rachel gulped. "You're right. We can't. Even though I'd love to see Katie Meadows eat a slug. . ."

Emily sighed, and started walking across the hall. Katie was unwrapping her sandwiches already, so there wasn't much time.

"What are you going to do?" Rachel whispered frantically, jogging after her.

"I don't know!" Emily hissed. But she could feel

the mirror in her pocket. It was warm, and she slipped her fingers round it for comfort. Sasha had said she would help. And she had Rachel with her. Two good friends, she realized suddenly, and the thought made Katie look less frightening.

Emily pulled up short by Katie's table, and Katie and Ellie-Mae and Lara stared at her.

"What do you want?" Katie demanded.

Emily said nothing. She certainly wasn't going to explain what Robin had done. She just reached down and snatched the sandwiches, and hurried away across the room.

"Oh, she's going to kill us," Rachel whispered. "She looks like she doesn't know whether to scream for a teacher or throw her water bottle at your head."

"I don't care. Whatever she does, if we'd let her eat a slug she'd have done something worse, wouldn't she?" Emily stuffed Katie's sandwiches down into the bin where they emptied the trays, burying them under leftover beans and bits of cottage pie. "There. She won't fish those out."

She hurried back to the end of the line, passing Robin, who glared at her furiously, and stood there staring at the floor tiles. Now it was just a case of waiting to see what Katie would do to get them back.

It was the waiting that was the worst part of it, Emily decided. All through the afternoon, Katie kept looking at her. Just a slow, steady stare that seemed to say, *You wait*. Emily wanted to stand up in the middle of the classroom and yell at her, just to make her do something, but she forced herself to smile sweetly back, as though she didn't care. *It only works if she thinks you're scared*, she told herself. *She only picks on people if they're scared of her.*

In the end, Katie waited until they were walking home. Emily supposed she should have worked that one out – it was the ideal chance for her to get them on their own, without any teachers around. She hadn't thought of it, though, because she knew that Katie's mother usually picked her up from school in the car. The girls had assumed that Katie was leaving them till tomorrow.

"They're following us," Robin said, nudging Emily with his elbow.

"Should we run?" Rachel asked nervously, glancing behind her.

Emily shook her head. She *was* scared of Katie (only someone with no sense wouldn't be) but she was a lot less scared than she had been before last night. Katie wasn't going to throw her lifeless body to a bunch of hunting hounds, after all. The mirror trembled in her pocket, and she pulled it out, glancing quickly down into it. Sasha was there, smiling at her, and Emily rubbed her thumb gently over the mirror glass, feeling a little tingle of magic. She had saved Sasha. She could deal with stupid Katie Meadows.

She stopped walking, and caught Rachel's arm to stop her too.

Rachel looked at her anxiously, her eyes round and pleading. She wanted to run away, Emily could tell.

"You don't have to stay," she whispered. "It's Robin's fault we got into this. Go home!"

"My fault!" Robin squeaked crossly. "*I* didn't get into a fight with Katie Meadows, I just helped you two out. You should have let her eat the sandwiches. You just wasted good slugs."

"I'm not going home," Rachel muttered out of the side of her mouth, as Katie and Ellie-Mae and Lara came closer. Emily and Rachel and Robin stood staring at them.

"Ahhh. You've got your little brother to protect you," Katie sneered.

Emily smiled at her thoughtfully. Katie had no idea what Robin could really do – except most of it he couldn't, of course, in case someone saw what he was.

But I could, someone said. Emily looked round, frowning, and then squeezed the mirror gently. She could hear Sasha, and it was obvious that none of the others could.

Because you're touching the mirror, I think. I can hear you too. Listen, Emily. Robin would get into trouble if he used magic, and he has to be careful not to let anyone see what he is. But no one knows that I'm here. I can protect you from them!

179

I suppose, Emily agreed. *What shall we do?*

She could feel Sasha laughing. *Let's wait and see.*

"What exactly did you think you were doing at lunchtime, Emily?" Katie snapped, glaring at the three of them.

Emily simply shrugged, and smiled at her. The smile was a bit forced to start with, but it got much easier to smile as she watched Katie seething. She *hated* it that Emily wasn't scared.

"You are so strange. Weird. Stealing sandwiches? Do you think that's clever now?" Katie sniggered, and the other two joined in dutifully, but Emily just smiled and smiled.

"What are you smiling like that for?" Katie

demanded. "Can't you talk? Honestly, I think she's lost her mind. . ." She whipped round to look at Rachel. "I'm not surprised, the way she hangs around with you all the time. She'd have to be stupid. You both are."

Rachel gulped and tried to say something, but only managed to get out a feeble little mutter. "Not stupid."

"What?" Katie sneered. "Say it again, cheese-brain."

Emily moved closer to Rachel, and flicked a glance at her and Robin. They were both looking at Katie; they wouldn't notice the mirror. She slipped it out of her pocket, and a wisp of silvery mist wove around her hand.

Make her take the mirror, Sasha said. *Hold it*

up so the light sparkles on the jewels. She'll want it.

Will you be all right? Emily worried, but she could feel the mirror dancing in her fingers. Sasha wanted to help. After the hopeless terror of the hunt, this was a way she could fight back. She let the sunlight sparkle on the mirror, as Sasha had told her.

"What's that?" Katie snatched at the glittery little thing and smirked at Emily. "I'll have this. As a swap for my sandwiches."

"But. . ." Rachel began to protest, but Emily caught her hand and squeezed, and she fell silent.

Katie turned the mirror over in her hands and peered into it.

182

Emily felt suddenly dizzy as Sasha's magic burst out of the mirror and wrapped itself round Katie, sealing her in a shimmery haze.

Katie's eyes widened, and she staggered a little, and the mirror fell from her hand, sunlight sparking off it as it turned over and over.

Emily swooped in and caught it before it hit the ground, and then stood back watching as Katie stared at her in horror.

Now she knows what she looks like, Sasha said, sounding a little smug. *The mirror showed her what everyone else sees. The bully. The mean girl that you all hate.*

Ellie-Mae and Lara were fussing over Katie, trying to get her to tell them what was the matter, but she didn't say anything. She pulled away from them and started to walk back up the road, staring at her feet.

"What's the matter with her?" Rachel whispered.

"I don't think she liked what she saw in the mirror," Emily told her, shrugging.

Once Robin had got her inside the house, he dragged Emily up to her bedroom.

"I've got homework, you know," Emily tried to say, but Robin only scowled.

"Shut up!" He slammed the bedroom door. "All right. Where is it?"

"What?" Emily widened her eyes and stared at him, but he was scaring her. He didn't look like her eight-year-old brother just now. His face was longer, and sharper, and his eyes were bigger. Any moment now, his wings were going to burst out of his back.

"Just give it to me!"

"I won't!" Emily snapped back, giving up the pretence. She felt too tired to argue with him, anyway. "Why should I?"

"Because it's dangerous, of course! If someone came through into the house who wasn't meant to, then they're dangerous!"

"She didn't just come through," Emily started to explain, but Robin had seen the mirror, still gripped in her hand, and he snatched it.

"I knew you had it hidden somewhere." He flung the little mirror down on the floor and pointed, his eyes glowing eerily green.

"Don't hurt her!" Emily yelled, trying to grab for the mirror, but Sasha was already misting out of it, standing on her bedroom floor – or just above it, actually – and eyeing Robin cautiously.

Robin stared at the silvery figure, and looked suddenly a lot less frightening and fairy-like. "I know you," he said accusingly. "You're that water sprite that used to look out of the mirror on the landing."

"Yes," Sasha agreed.

"What are you doing here? Did you come through the mirror? You could be in trouble, you know. No one's supposed to go through the doors. And how did you, anyway? They're meant to be sealed."

"It was me," Emily said apologetically. "She was being chased. When I went to the art gallery with school yesterday, I saw a painting, and she was in it."

"Who was chasing you? Hunters?" Robin asked, frowning.

"You knew about them?" Emily demanded. "They were going to let their hounds eat her! I can't believe that's allowed."

Robin only shook his head at her. "It was the hunters, then?" he asked Sasha.

"Yes."

"What did you do? Why were they after you?"

Sasha sighed. "Because I showed your sisters the door, when they were running from the Ladies."

187

"I had to help her," Emily told him, her eyes pleading. "Don't you see?"

"I suppose," Robin muttered. Lark and Lory hadn't taken him with them to rescue Emily, and he still minded. "But what's she going to do now? If she goes back, they'll be on her scent again."

"They wouldn't have given up, once they couldn't find her?" Emily asked hopefully, rubbing a hand across her eyes. "It's been nearly a whole day."

"They never give up," both the fairies said together, and Emily sighed. She was so tired, she felt suddenly desperate to sleep. She slumped down next to Robin, leaning against the door, and gazed exhaustedly at Sasha glittering in the light from the window.

"You'll have to stay here," she murmured, forcing the words out past the dreadful weariness. What was the matter with her? "I know it must be awful to be dragged away from everything, but you can't go back."

Sasha shivered, like dust motes dancing in the light, and then she darted suddenly towards the mirror, which was still lying on the floor.

"I must hide! They're coming!"

Emily tried to make herself care – to get up, to stand with Sasha and help protect them all. But she couldn't move.

"Who's coming?" she heard Robin demand. "They can't be – the hunters couldn't get through the doors."

"They don't need to – look at Emily! She's

dreaming again – they'll just follow the same dream-path we used, through there!" Sasha pointed at the windows, and Emily caught a last glimpse of the forest growing up around the palace, and flashes of white as the hounds poured through the trees. Then her eyes began to close.

She was leaning sleepily against Robin's shoulder now, fighting against the weariness that her settled through her, weighing her down like a chain. Somehow she couldn't fight against it enough to worry about Sasha and Robin.

Robin. She could feel him shaking her fiercely. Her eyelids flickered, and she saw mists growing, trailing through the trees, little wisps coiling out into her room. Soon the hounds would come racing through them, the mist coiling round their paws.

"Emily, wake up! They're too strong for me to stop. You dreamed your way to rescue Sasha, and now the hunters are chasing you both back through the dream. You have to wake up now! There's not time for me to get anyone to help; they'll get Sasha any moment. The mirror's no good – they'll just track her to it and smash it."

"Can't. . . Too tired. . ." she murmured, her eyes closing again as the figures in green began to follow the hounds out through the dark trees in the window glass.

"I can't wake her!" Robin said over her head, and she heard Sasha sigh.

"You'd better take her out. Get away from here. It's only me that they're after. Don't let them catch you too."

"But Emily's the one bringing them," Robin muttered. "She'll let them into the house. Mum said she was going to make sure Emily's dreams were guarded. I don't understand."

Emily flinched and wriggled against his shoulder, trying to pull herself out of the dream. She was in amongst the trees now, and her bedroom was strangely laid over them, like a drawing on thin paper. She could hear the hounds baying, and she *knew*, she knew how to stop them, if she could only wake up enough.

The first hound was racing towards her, his white paws muddied and his ears flying as he sped between the trees. She could see his teeth glinting, and the redness of his tongue.

She had to wake up!

Sasha was crouching next to her now, with her arms round Emily's shoulders. "I can see the hounds. They're coming for us!"

Emily flung herself away from Robin and Sasha, reaching out towards the bed, her fingers clutching frantically at the covers. "Emily, stop them!" Robin howled.

"She's half awake," she heard Sasha say as she stretched out her fingers more desperately. "What's she doing? Oh, the bed! Emily told me, your mother, Lady Eva, she laid a spell on the bed. Drag her across to it!"

Emily felt Robin and Sasha grab her, and

193

then all at once she was wrapped in the cool freshness of the spell, as if her mother was stroking her hair. The magic smelled of her mother, of citrus and spices, and it wrapped lovingly around Emily. She heard Robin gasp in relief, and felt Sasha's panicked fingers loosen from round her arm.

"They've lost the scent. . ." the water-fairy whispered. "Look!"

A strange, furious howling echoed in Emily's ears. Sniffing, and scuffling paws, and the angry shouting of the men, as they argued over the sudden disappearance of the scent.

Then the howling of the hounds died away, and Emily was awake again, leaning back against her bed.

"Are they gone?" she whispered hoarsely, looking back at Robin and Sasha, who were kneeling beside her.

"Your mother's spell turned them away," Sasha told her. The frightened shadows on her face seemed to have died away, and she looked younger. Her hair was coiling around her shoulders as though water was running through it, and her eyes were bright.

"They won't come back?"

Sasha shook her head. "The spell was very strong. It destroyed the scent. They could only pick it up again if I go back."

"Then you won't," Emily said flatly. "You'll stay. I'll explain to Mum and Dad," she added quickly to Robin, who looked as though he was about to argue. "It's like I said before, she has to! I'm not letting her go back and be eaten!"

Robin shook his head. "I know. We can't send her back."

"Do you need a river?" Emily asked worriedly. "I mean, there is one, not far from here, but there are people fishing, and walking dogs all the time. It might be difficult to hide in."

Sasha frowned. "I can sense water very close by. Still water, but clean."

Robin snorted with laughter. "That's the pond! You can't live in the pond!"

"I could. . ." Sasha smiled at him and stretched out her arms. Her pale skin seemed to thin, so that she was almost transparent and rippling like water. And then she was simply gone.

196

Emily stared down at the drops of water glittering on the boards of her bedroom floor, and laughed. "She's gone!"

"Only back into the mirror." Robin pointed to the tiny, jewelled circle, which had been kicked almost under the bed. "So you can take her downstairs. I can't believe you're actually going to put a water-sprite in the pond. Good luck explaining that to Mum and Dad." He peered down into the glass. "What about the goldfish?"

Sasha gazed up at him. "I like fish. . ." she told him sweetly, her greenish eyes glinting in the surface of the glass.

"That's what I'm worried about!"

"She won't eat the fish!" Emily said, rolling her

197

eyes at him. She stood up slowly, the weariness of the dream-spell still lingering a little. But then she smiled to herself. Dad and Robin had been right – somehow, somewhere inside her, was just a little spark of magic. Enough to force herself into another world, and rescue a friend. Emily might not be a fairy like the rest of her family, but she almost didn't mind.

She cupped the mirror gently in her fingers, and went to the door, walking slowly, still a little dreamily, through the house and out into the sunlit garden.

Then, by the smooth, dark water of the pond, she crouched down in the grass, her eyes caught by the gentle waving of the water-weed, clinging to the rocks.

"Can you really live here?" she whispered to Sasha, stroking the edge of the mirror.

But already the water-sprite was misting eagerly out of the glass, her fingers stretching towards the water. It seemed to know she was there, the surface breaking into a hundred sparkling circles as she dabbled in her fingertips.

"Ah. . ." she breathed, dipping one hand in deeper, and then all of a sudden she was gone. Emily couldn't remember afterwards what she had seen in that split second when Sasha dived — a brightly-feathered waterbird, or an otter, its pelt glittering with water droplets. Or just a girl, her silver dress patterned with a hundred different gleaming leaves.

Thank you, the plants around the water rustled

and whispered, and Emily leaned over watching the glittering ripples. *I'll see you soon.*

Emily trailed her fingers across the surface of the water, and smiled, feeling the magic all around her.

HOLLY has always loved animals. As a child, she had two dogs, a cat, and at one point, nine gerbils (an accident). Holly's other love is books. Holly now lives in Reading with her husband, three sons and a very spoilt cat.

Look out for Emily's next adventure

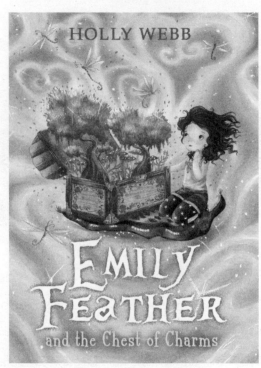

HOLLY WEBB

EMILY
FEATHER
and the Chest of Charms

COMING SOON!